J SF
Daley, Michael J.
Shanghaied to the moon /
New York : G. P. Putnam's Sons,
c2007.

SHANGHAIED TO THE MOON

MICHAEL J. DALEY

G. P. PUTNAM'S SONS · NEW YORK

G.P. PUTNAM'S SONS

A division of Penguin Young Readers Group.

Published by The Penguin Group.

Penguin Group (USA) Inc., 375 Hudson Street, New York, NY 10014, U.S.A.

Penguin Group (Canada), 90 Eglinton Avenue East, Suite 700, Toronto, Ontario, Canada M4P 2Y3 (a division of Pearson Penguin Canada Inc.).

Penguin Books Ltd, 80 Strand, London WC2R 0RL, England.

Penguin Ireland, 25 St. Stephen's Green, Dublin 2, Ireland (a division of Penguin Books Ltd.).

Penguin Group (Australia), 250 Camberwell Road, Camberwell, Victoria 3124, Australia (a division of Pearson Australia Group Pty Ltd).

Penguin Books India Pvt Ltd, 11 Community Centre, Panchsheel Park, New Delhi - 110 017, India.

Penguin Group (NZ), Cnr Airborne and Rosedale Roads, Albany, Auckland 1310, New Zealand (a division of Pearson New Zealand Ltd).

Penguin Books (South Africa) (Pty) Ltd, 24 Sturdee Avenue, Rosebank, Johannesburg 2196, South Africa.

Penguin Books Ltd, Registered Offices: 80 Strand, London WC2R 0RL, England.

Published simultaneously in Canada. Printed in the United States of America.

Design by Marikka Tamura. Text set in Times Europa.

Library of Congress Cataloging-in-Publication Data

Daley, Michael J.

Shanghaied to the moon / Michael J. Daley.

p. cm.

Summary: Desperate to become a space pilot like his mother, despite his father's opposition, thirteen-year-old Stewart meets an old spacer who offers him the chance to learn AstroNav during a flight to the moon in the year 2065—and reveals some family secrets along the way.

[1. Space flight—Fiction. 2. Memory—Fiction. 3. Adventure and adventurers. 4. Science fiction.]

I. Title. PZ7.D15265Sha 2007 [Fic]—dc22 2006020532

ISBN 978-0-399-24619-7

1 3 5 7 9 10 8 6 4 2

First Impression

*For Jessie Haas
who always believed
and Tim Travaglini
who proved her right
—MJD*

MISSION TIME

T minus 16 (hours):00 (minutes):01 (seconds)

TOMORROW'S my birthday and my father is on the Moon.

That's no coincidence. Two days ago, Dad blasted off to do an emergency job for Alldrives, the biggest aerospace company in the solar system. He didn't have to go. A thousand other computer network specialists could've handled the job. Nope, Dad went to the Moon to get away from me.

Through the window in the Counselor's waiting room, I watch as the Moon slips between the perfect line where the sky meets the ocean. It's a daytime rising and the gigantic orb is pale, almost ghostly. It seems to linger at the threshold of the sky as if someone is holding it back, then it breaks free to claim all of space for itself.

Makes me shiver.

Like an enormous opaque bubble, the Moon rises higher above the Old Spaceport out on the end of the peninsula. I can barely make out the big dimple of Copernicus Crater. Invisible, Luna Base rests at the rim. Dad's staying there.

The only thing I want for my thirteenth birthday is his signature on my application to Space Academy Camp, which is due next week. I had a whole new round of arguments about why I should go all planned out, but now he's gone.

I turn my back on the window. No one else is in the waiting room. No one is in with the Counselor ahead of me, either. But the sign above the office door still says, "STEWART, WAIT, PLEASE." Everybody's acting weird. The Counselor never makes me wait.

I take a seat.

If you ask me, Dad ought to be sitting here. Mark, too. He's like an old mother hen with Dad gone. I mean, he called to make this appointment at two o'clock in the morning! The dream wasn't that bad, as my dreams go, even if Mark says I woke up screaming.

My feet jiggle. A few more minutes and I'm outta here. I have a science project due tomorrow that I haven't even started.

I snug my portable 3-Vid goggles and earphones over my head and select a capsule at random from the cluster of Val Thorsten adventures in my pocket. When I pop the capsule into the earpiece, virtual reality takes over. The waiting room becomes the bridge of a spaceship, the *Predator* from Asteroid Run. The engines throb, a deep bass note in my bones. There's the smell of people in a tight space. I'm stationed at weapons control.

Not ten feet away stands the captain, Val Thorsten; tall, muscled, his long blond hair swept back into the classic pilot's ponytail. Leadership radiates from him like a force. It's easy to imagine his Viking ancestors on the foredeck, awash in the spray of a stormy ocean, guiding their ships to new worlds.

The voice-over begins: "Pirates have been raiding ships throughout the asteroid belt, then escaping—"

Asteroid Run isn't one of Val's best adventures. There's only one really exciting part. I hit *fast-forward*.

Fast-forward in virtual reality is wild. The world squiggles. I don't like to use it. It reminds me too much about why I've been seeing the Counselor since Mom died. The squiggly effect is a lot like what happens just before a flashback hits me. Sometimes a word, or sound, or smell will trigger one. One second I'm living a normal life, the next things kind of shimmer around the edges and—wham!—I'm in a waking nightmare.

I haven't had a squiggly in months. That's why I don't just cut out on the Counselor. The Counselor helps keep them away.

I hit *play*. At least with a 3-Vid, I know I'll drop back into the same story . . .

. . . and we're in hot pursuit of a vicious-looking pirate ship: all cruel angles and Z-blasters. It plunges into a dense cluster of asteroid rubble. We blaze in after it. One wrong move and those flinty rocks will shred us into confetti.

Three other pirate ships shimmer into view on the main screen.

Ambush!

They open fire. My teeth chatter. My ears ring. Alarms blare.

We're hit!

Another volley pounds the hull like a thousand hammers on a gong. The deck pitches. Vertigo grips me. In the real world, my arm flies out. Knuckles smack hard against the empty seat next to me in the waiting room. Good thing no one else is here. Shouldn't watch 3-Vids in public.

"NavComp damaged!" Tony, the chief engineer, shouts. "We have to stop or we'll be smashed to pieces!"

"And let them capture us? Never. Let me have her, Bob." Val leaps into the pilot's seat. Bob's a good pilot, great even, but he's not the greatest. Val's hands flutter over the helm console. The ship responds, engines purring like a stroked cat. We hurtle between the clustered rocks. Dance around death. The *Predator* breaks into clear space. Val takes us through a loop the loop, then shoves the throttle to the max, leaving the pirates lost in the rocks.

I yank off the goggles, stung by the beauty of Val's skill and mad at Dad all over again. Why is he ruining my chance to do that? Unless he lets me go to Space Academy Camp, I'll never get to be a rocket pilot like Val. I can do all kinds of advanced aeronautics, but not basic AstroNav. It's humiliating. Camp is my last hope. They have the best AstroNav training program in the solar system. Even a few chimps have passed.

I know I'm smarter than a chimp.

Bing.

With that little chime, the sign changes: "ENTER, PLEASE."

Mrs. Phillips isn't in the office. The huge view screen on the wall behind the empty desk declares:

MRS. PHILLIPS REGRETS SHE CANNOT APPEAR IN PERSON, STEWART. AUTOMATED SIMULATION IS DOWNLOADING.

Too bad. I'd get out of here faster with Mrs. Phillips. She's my human counselor. The Counselor is an artificial intelligence program. It's more rigorous than Mrs. Phillips. I have to be careful what I tell it.

We could waste the afternoon chasing associations around the rings of Saturn!

I sit on the stool in front of the desk. The holofield shimmers into the empty chair and becomes a perfect live-action image of Mrs. Phillips, right down to the three red hairs that grow out of the mole on her cheek. On the wall behind the hologram is a large view screen containing the machine's sensors. They warm up, murmuring like a crowded room.

Sometimes I imagine a bunch of psychologists are behind that screen controlling what the Counselor does and says. But the machine never acts like a real person. It's never warm and caring like Mrs. Phillips.

"Hello, Stewart," the hologram says. "Sorry I'm a simulation. That was pretty short notice."

"Yeah, well, Mark got rattled. He's been awfully jumpy lately. And Dad, too. It's like living with two sticks of dynamite. Did you know Dad's on the Moon?"

"We are aware of that."

"You are?"

"Why do you sound so surprised?"

"Because Mark and I wouldn't even know if I hadn't found the space suit. Dad said the job was in Australia."

I'd snuck into Dad's room to slip his Megaplexor tool back into its case before he could find it missing and the suit was lying on the bed like a puddle of mercury: one of the new ultralight models. I remember the cobweb lightness of the material as I pulled it through my hand; how it reflected back my own body heat when I draped it over my shoulders.

"Don't you think it's weird Dad going to the Moon and trying to hide that from us? Mark burst an O-ring when he found out. He kept yelling about Dad postponing something again. Do you know what he meant?"

"We have discussed the incident with your brother."

"Oh." Sometimes I forget that I'm not the only one in my family who needs counseling. "So you've seen Mark?"

"Earlier today." The holo image smiles. "But this is your session, Stewart. Please tell us why you found your father's actions weird."

"Dad doesn't *do* space! Ever since Mom's crash. He won't even go to the space museum with me. It's totally weird for him to blast off without a moment's notice. What if he doesn't get back in time to sign my application to—"

"That conflict is not the subject of your visit." The image leans its elbows on the desk. "Tell us about the dream."

Mrs. Phillips might come around in front of the

desk to hear a bad dream. Definitely, she'd pay more attention to what's really bothering me.

"Actually, it gave me a neat idea for my science project, which is due tomorrow. So can I go now?"

"Tell us the dream."

"Okay. Fine." What a pain! Now we'll have to analyze it. "I was on this rolling surface . . . all silver and gray. There was a black shoe box, but something red caught my eye first. When I picked it up, the red bit was a miniature door, shaped just like a cockpit door in a passenger shuttle. I thought I heard voices, you know, in the box. Lots of them. They . . . the voices . . . they wanted me to open the door. And then I thought I heard . . . Mom's voice . . . inside and I tried to open it, but—I woke up. Mark said I was screaming. I don't remember that."

The image sits frozen; analyzing. Right now, I wish it were Mrs. Phillips. She'd care that remembering the dream has upset me. It's much creepier than it seemed in the night.

"Your birthday is soon, isn't it?" the Counselor says. "You'll be thirteen?"

"You know exactly when my birthday is. Why are you changing the subject? Is the dream that bad?"

"A birthday is an exciting day." The image smiles. "It can also be a difficult day for someone who has lost their mother."

"You're obsessed with Mom. She's not the problem. Dad is. And AstroNav. I'll never be a rocket pilot without AstroNav. I have to take the entrance exams to Space Academy while I'm thirteen. That means this year! I'll never be able to pass if I don't get to camp first—"

"You have explained the details in previous sessions."

"Well, the way you keep changing the subject makes me think you never pay attention."

"We are always aware. Are you planning a party?"

"You're ignoring my real problem! Only the very best get into Space Academy. Julio and Tanner and Caytlyn all want to be pilots, too. I'm competing with them!"

"We know of your classmates' aspirations. Are you inviting them to your party?"

I give up. Even *I* can't outstubborn a machine. "Yeah."

"Mark mentioned that he and Andrea will be baking you a cake. That's very nice of them."

"I guess."

"You don't sound too happy about that. Does Mark having a girlfriend trouble you at all?"

"No." I like Andrea, but if I told the Counselor why, it would just say I was off subject again. *She* thinks my wanting to be a pilot is a kind of calling, like ministers get for the church. Dad acts like I have a disease. And Mark—well, lately there's been Andrea, so he's not paying much attention to me.

"Girlfriends become wives, then mothers. Perhaps she reminds you of your loss and that brings pain?"

"Aren't *I* supposed to do the associating?"

"Very well." The image folds its hands primly on the desk. The sensors behind the screen whir, adjusting for close observation. "We are all ears."

Machine ears, machine eyes focus on me. I don't like how it keeps bringing up Mom. It's probing for something. But what? When it gets chatty like this, I have to be careful what I say.

Sometimes Mom's death seems so unreal to me that I imagine she's away on a long haul to the moons of Jupiter. Any day, she'll walk through our apartment door. She'll take me by the hand and say, "Come on, Stub. Let's go to the Old Spaceport. I've got a rocket to show you."

The Counselor would call that an unhealthy fantasy. But sometimes, it's better than anything the Counselor can do for me.

I shift on the hard seat. "Can I go now?"

"This is a critical time, Stewart." Mrs. Phillips's image takes on a somber, disapproving expression. "Perhaps, before you rush off, we should review past events that may be a source of pain for you?"

The Counselor's talking about the NewsVid. It hasn't shown that to me in *ages*. How can it be so off course? "Watching that won't help. I'm not thinking about Mom. I'm mad at Dad. He's ruining my life!"

"It has helped. It will help." The image shimmers, then fades away around a sad smile, leaving a clear view of the screen on the wall behind the desk. "Watch, please."

Maybe the bad dream connects in a way only the Counselor can understand? Maybe I'd better pay attention.

The old NewsVid detailing the last minutes of Frisco Shuttle Flight 78 begins. I know it better than many of my Val Thorsten 3-Vids. The view is of a pale blue sky crowded with cotton ball clouds. The camera moves, seeking the incoming passenger shuttle. The chatter between Tower Control and the pilot is calm. Shuttle landings are routine events, repeated a dozen times a day.

The camera pans the crowd and there I am, a short, auburn-haired boy beside my tall dad, my tall brother Mark, the basketball star. I'm short even for a six-year-old. The camera stays focused on us for a long time. Pretty boring really. I can never figure why the news crew wasted so much time watching us. I'd rather see the shuttle. What was Mom doing just before it happened?

A sharp sputter of static erupts from the NewsVid. My breath catches and I can't help but pay attention. Tower Control says, "Contact lost with incoming."

The camera moves urgently now, its electro-mechanical optics straining just as the human eyes strain. The screen fills with an image of the mysteriously stricken passenger shuttle, upside down, wobbling in a rocklike dive toward the hard earth.

I grab the edge of the stool. Bile stings like grapefruit juice at the back of my throat.

"Eyes open, please."

The camera is on the boy again. His mother, the famous rocket pilot, is on that shuttle. She was only a passenger, returning from a trip to the Moon. But now she is called upon to take over for the blinded pilot. To fly her toughest mission yet. Raw fear shows in the upturned face of the boy.

I can't bring that feeling back into my own body. I can't remember the terror. The Counselor has explained that the combination of youth and shock has dulled my memory: a kind of self-protective reflex of the mind.

A good thing, really, but that . . . absence . . . makes the NewsVid seem more like a bad 3-Vid; too stingy on the special effects. Just *once* I'd like to really remember the feel of the cool air on my face, the hush of the crowd, the biting chemical stink of the crash foam in my nose. Feel Mark and Dad pressing against me as they're doing now in the picture. Hear the soft whistling sound of the massive, too-quickly-falling shuttle.

I wish the camera spent more time watching the shuttle. What was Mom up against? What systems were damaged? What was working? How did she even get into the pilot's seat from the ceiling?

I've tried flying upside down in the simulator. It's really hard! The belts bite into your shoulders. All the controls work opposite and backward. You have to fight every instinct, every bit of common sense, or you'll make the wrong maneuver.

I rise up off the stool. The miraculous moment is coming. The shuttle abruptly flips upright. Mom's triumphant cry rings out in the office. "Tower, tower, positive airfoil! I've got control!"

Whatever she was faced with in there, she was handling it. But then something went wrong. Maybe she made a mistake. Or another system blew. Or maybe, with the hydraulics out, she wasn't strong enough to work the yoke.

In the best of my dreams, I'm there with her. Not a six-year-old. I'm Val Thorsten and I reach into the cockpit. Grab the yoke. Put my hand over hers. Pull! Pull! The scar across my palm hurts from pressing against the yoke, but I just pull harder.

"Eyes open! You must watch."

I want to stay in my head . . . where it ends different—
    the lightning reflex
    the brilliant last-second maneuver
    even the cavalry
    anything.
    Because the hero shouldn't die in the end.

2

MISSION TIME

T minus 14:42:02

I take the elevator from the Counselor's office to the TransHub, hail a Marble, and get in. When I press my thumb to the fare plate, the Marble rolls down the chute to the main travel tube. Dozens of Marbles whiz by like beads on a string, while mine bobs gently in the levitation field.

"Destination please?"

I should go home. Get to work on my science project.

"I'm sorry. Perhaps I did not hear you. Destination please?"

The neat idea for the project is gone. It was clear as a blueprint before.

"If you do not wish to take a ride, please return to the TransHub. If you do not wish . . ."

Mark won't even be home yet. He was going to the cafe with Andrea.

"If you . . ."

"Gamma Station, Old Spaceport."

"Thank you."

The Marble drops into the traffic stream and accelerates, but the motion dampers are so good there's no feeling of speed. That's what I don't like about Marbles. You can barely tell the difference between parked or moving. I want to feel the punch of acceleration.

"ETA is four minutes under present traffic conditions."

My mind slips into automatic, calculating the average speed at 120.345 miles per hour. The Marble's readout says 120.348. I'm that quick on my feet with calculations, but it doesn't help with AstroNav. My problem is getting the star field vectors oriented right. It's like I have some kind of stellar dyslexia.

The Marble stops at Gamma Station. The door snaps open. A chill ocean breeze whisks all the heat out. I zip up my jacket and step onto the platform. No one here, except a guy asleep on a bench in the sun next to the outside wall of the station. He's hugging a large, limp duffel bag. Its dark shape looks like a giant toy bear with all the stuffing kicked out.

Angling away from the bench, I put about ten feet

between myself and the guy. An easy scissors-kick vault puts me over the guardrail in front of the fence. I lean against the wire mesh. The metal bites cold where it touches my face. Rays of the late afternoon sun seep through my jacket, warming my back.

The Old Spaceport spreads out eastward over the salt marshes to the ocean. Ships aren't launched from here anymore. It's a museum. When I want action, I go to the New Canaveral Spaceport further up the coast. Even from here, I can see some of the taller gantries and watch a few ships come and go. Dad's rocket left from there two nights ago—an Alldrives Eniex 70. It can make the Moon run in four hours; nothing but the best for employees of Alldrives Space Systems.

That's who Val Thorsten works for. Who I want to work for. They run the asteroid mines and the Jupiter colonies and eighty percent of the transports. They build the fastest ships and win the exploration contracts. That's where I want to be, on the edge, piloting that kind of ship into unknown space. Ships like the ones displayed here at the Old Spaceport.

They were all unique in their day—firsts of a kind. Each one needed a special pilot. Apollo vehicles are over to the right. Off to the left is a Jupiter Floater; Mom was the test pilot for the prototype. In the center, the Lance Ramjet perches on its pedestal, angled toward the stars. The hull glints orange in the sunlight. It might have glowed like that when Val Thorsten skimmed it through the clouds of Venus.

Venus: Inferno Below the Clouds is my favorite of his 3-Vid adventures. It was Val's first mission for Alldrives; a test to see if this young hotshot fresh out of the academy really had what it took to become a permanent member of their team.

The best part is when the Lance Ramjet is halfway through the Venusian atmosphere. The alarms start singing. The cloud density is above spec. The engines are in danger of flaming out. Abort! But it's too late. Val's plunging toward the lava-hot surface, out of control, with only a few minutes to find a way to refire the engines or . . . well, I wouldn't have a pocket full of his other adventures if he hadn't succeeded.

That Lance Ramjet is no replica. Val pulled it out. Val Thorsten always pulls it out.

"Hey!" A voice. Close. "You a kid or a midget?"

"Heeii-yaa!" I spin around, crouch into Position One, on my toes, jigging, ready for anything.

The man from the bench leans on the guardrail a few feet from me. He's bent so far over I see more of the top of his balding head than his face. A fringe of silver hair above his ears is pulled back into a knobby ponytail. Looks like the frayed end of a rope.

"Nice reflexes." He straightens up, winces, and

grabs at the small of his back. "Damn Mother Earth. No place for a spacer."

A spacer? He wears his stub of a ponytail like a pilot. And that *is* a flight jacket. Frayed bits of thread faintly outline less grimy patches on the sleeve and chest where the insignias used to be. The zipper is broken open over his big belly. He doesn't look like a real pilot to me.

"Drop the ninja act." His teeth flash white and even as he speaks. "I'm the guy you came to see."

What's he talking about? I deepen my crouch. He stares at me staring at him. His face is broad-featured. His mouth cuts a cheerless line across it.

"Pad 12?" He frowns. Rubs at the silver stubble on his jaw. "You *are* here about my ad, aren't you?"

"Ad? What ad?"

Disappointment remolds his face. He turns his back to me and, with a groan, settles his butt on the rail. He sure is hurting. They've mostly got the bone problem solved today, but a lot of people who went to space a few decades ago have serious troubles. Normal gravity can be torture.

Most old spacers never come back to Earth, not without a really good reason. He's probably a nutter. Just some homeless guy with bad arthritis who *thinks* he's a spacer.

"Um . . . mister?"

"You still here?" His head half turns my way.

"Yeah."

"Come round where I can see you."

I one-step over the guardrail, but keep my distance, just to be safe, though I doubt he has any moves I couldn't handle. I have three years of karate under my belt.

He rests his hands on his knees. Short breaths whisper through his parted lips. He runs his tongue over their cracked dryness. "Well?"

"You got a place? I mean, you don't sleep on that bench all night, do you?"

"So what if I do?" He juts his chin at me.

"Well, maybe I could help. Rent you a cubby—"

"I've got a berth. That's not my problem." He reaches into the right pocket and pulls out a small squeeze bottle—the kind they use in zero-g. The contents glow amber in the sun. He pops the straw in his mouth, squirts. The sharp smell of alcohol comes to my nose on the breeze.

"So what is your problem?" I ask, though I'm probably looking at it in that bottle.

"Ever been to space, kid?"

"Have *you*?" Why should I give a straight answer if he doesn't?

He draws a tight circle in the air with the bottle. "Done a few loops."

"That jacket looks Salvation Army to me."

"Because of this?" He pulls at a few threads. "Did that myself."

"Why?"

"That's a long story, and I'm in no mood to tell it." He reaches deep into the left pocket, looks surprised to find something in there. He brings out a fistful of insignias. "Want 'em?"

He opens his hand. I snag the biggest one as the rest flutter to the ground. My fingers trace rich textured weaving that forms the letters *TE*. Never heard of an outfit with those call letters.

"What's TE?" I pick up the rest. Tuck them in my pocket.

"Before your time, kid." He takes another drink, then, twisting carefully around, points with the bottle. "You know that ship? In the center?"

"Sure! That's the Lance Ramjet. I just saw the remake of Venus: Inferno Below the Clouds. Have you seen it?"

"Yeah. The original."

"You *have* to see the remake. They really improved the sense-o-rama. Your teeth chatter when the Lance Ramjet hits the clouds!"

"Chatter?" He makes a disgusted face. "That's nothing, kid. Those engines. Kick your butt between your eyeballs."

"Someday I'll feel that. Someday, I'm going to Pluto."

"Pluto, huh? No one's dared since the Valadium Thruster failed."

"I'm not afraid to try again . . . only . . . I might never get the chance. I can't do AstroNav."

"Bigger problem, kid. No ship."

"Someone could build another Valadium Thruster. I'd take it out there."

"Why would you want to do that? She . . . didn't make it." He tips the bottle back, squeezes long and hard.

"I've studied the design. Got some ideas of what might have gone wrong."

He's about to take another drink. Stops himself. "Gimme a for instance."

Is he baiting me? The other kids love to get me talking about the Valadium Thruster, then poke fun at me for caring so much about a ship that fell into the sun. But he's waiting with an interested look.

"My best guess: Something went wrong with the impulsor engines during the Whip maneuver. Maybe . . ." He'll laugh now, if he's going to. "Maybe even caused a transdimensional shift."

"Interesting." He rotates the bottle in his palm. For a few long moments, he seems to be hypnotized by the way the sunlight winks off the faceted surface. "And if that's really what went wrong, you could fix it?"

"With the right team, yeah. If only Val hadn't lost it in . . ." It's too painful to say out loud. The image from the 3-Vid Pluto: A Star too Far comes harshly into my mind. The beautiful Valadium Thruster melting to lava as it plunges toward the sun.

"Something to dream about, anyway."

"You sound like my dad. I don't want to dream. I want to do it!"

"I can make that happen for you." He looks straight at me. His eyes are the pale blue of a morning sky. The irises are as dark as space.

I don't look away. My determination is mirrored in that darkness. "How?"

"How tall are you?"

"Huh?"

"Tall, you know, feet, inches."

This guy changes the subject as often as the Counselor.

"Why do you want to know that?"

"To qualify." He looks away, suddenly sounding indifferent. "No point in telling you any more if you don't."

Whatever this guy wants, it isn't going to be me. I'm always too short. But I make myself answer. "I'm four three and nine sixteenths."

He breathes in deep, lets it go slow. His head nods the slightest bit down, then up. "Good enough."

"For what?"

"Got a little trip to the Moon in the works. Need a cabin boy," he says, still not looking at me. "Have you been to space? You never said."

Seems the qualifying tests aren't over. This'll be the end. "No, but I've seen hundreds of 3-Vids. I've done an entire Apollo Moon mission in the simulator. The eight-hour version."

"Woo-eee!" He hoots. "Eight hours in a ground can and we are going to Pluto!"

"I wanted to do the longer version, but I'm too young!"

"Cool your jets, kid. No offense. Just a bit tame by my standards, that's all. Did you pilot the LEM?"

Guessing the next question, I nod reluctantly. I always do the toughest simulation, the actual flight path of the first Moon landing. Even the legendary Neil Armstrong had trouble when he had to go manual with less than a minute of fuel left.

"How'd the landing go?"

I'm tempted to lie, to claim some of Armstrong's

glory for myself, but the truth has gotten me this far. "Crashed."

"Honest. I like that."

He pushes up the cuff of his jacket, exposing a Chronomatrix. It's a watch/supercomputer combo popular with pilots—about fifty years ago! You can order a replica from the Val Thorsten fan club. I never wear mine except for play. It's not network compatible like the OmniLink on my wrist.

He flicks a function button with his little finger. "Damn, missed the window. Come back tomorrow. An hour earlier."

"Window? *Launch* window?"

"Bingo. Pad 12, remember?" He gestures toward the coast. I can just make out the silhouette of the gantry at Pad 12. It looks like a dead pine tree against the hazy horizon. The rocket isn't visible from here, but I've explored all the derelicts, so I know it's an ancient Personal Launch Vehicle. PLVs are designed to do one thing—get people into orbit and docked to a spaceship or space station. No frills.

Suddenly, all the excitement building in me turns sour. I feel like a fool for taking this crazy old bum seriously.

"Thanks for nothing, mister. That old thing can't fly."

"It can now," he says. "I overhauled the booster with a NitriLox regenerator."

I take another long look at the PLV. A NitriLox regen would do it. I look at him tilting back the bottle again. He may be a drunk with an old watch, but that's cutting-edge tech. How'd he get his hands on it?

"So what do you say, kid? Good opportunity to learn a little AstroNav . . ." His sloppy grin turns into a kind of leer and alarm bells start going off in my head, like when a simulation is going bad. Never take candy from a stranger!

"You didn't plan this trip to teach me AstroNav. What's the mission? And what's being short got to do with it?"

"The mission . . ." He glances around, nervous, worried about the hidden mikes and cameras of TIA. The government's Total Information Awareness security system would certainly keep an eye on a public space like this. It would notice a guy like him for sure. He probably stole that regenerator.

He takes a quick sip. Licks his lips. "I left a piece of my life up there, kid. I need your help to get it back."

I can't keep from glancing at the bottle.

"Don't worry about this. Just medicine for my bones."

"Nobody *has* to drink."

"By Jupiter, I got me a Boy Scout!"

"I'm not a Boy Scout. We learned in school. The Counselors can help you with that kind of problem."

"Oh sure, kid. Counselors can make you forget. But some pain—you hang on to it!" He snatches a fistful of air. "Fruit of your life."

"Make you forget?"

"Bitter fruit." He takes a swig, then swipes a sleeve across his mouth.

"What do you mean, they can make you forget?"

"Bit of advice, kid. You want to be the best, better than Vaaaaal Thorsten?!" He rolls out the name like a trumpet fanfare went along with it. "Huh? Do you?"

"More than anything."

"The instincts. The reflexes. Nobody knows how the old noodle"—he taps his temple—"puts it all together. So stay away from Counselors. Never let them mess with your head."

"Stay away? But I *have* to see them. I get . . . I need . . . I mean, I have bad dreams."

"Not my problem. Just be here tomorrow." He dismisses me with a sweep of the bottle. "Go on, beat it. Got some counseling of my own to do."

3

mission time

T minus 12:37:03

CABIN BOY NEEDED for Moon mission. Must be
under 4'5" tall. Various duties. AstroNav lessons. Free
passage to the Moon. Report in person to Pad 12,
Old Spaceport, New Canaveral, FL. (Midgets also con-
sidered.)

This is the one and only hit the computer finds. It's in
Spacefarer Magazine, the official aerospace journal of
record. The old spacer wasn't pulling my leg.

First time being short has won me any prizes.

I look up at the gigantic glow-in-the-dark Moon
map pasted to the ceiling over my bed. Models of all
Val Thorsten's ships hang around the big circle. A tap
on the Lance Ramjet sets it whirling on its wire. It
smacks a long, sweeping heat radiator of the

Valadium Thruster. I quickly steady the ships. Can't let the VT get scratched.

Flopping onto the bed, I stare up at Copernicus Crater. Wouldn't it just blow Dad's mind if I showed up on the Moon? He'd have to sign my application then or I'd threaten never to come back. Maybe I'd never come back anyway.

What kind of ship might the old spacer have parked in orbit? A Comet Catcher? A Neutron Slider?

Right. And his berth is at the Ritz!

Of course, there *are* stories of rich people who pretend to be poor. Eccentrics. He must have *some* money if he could afford a NitriLox regenerator for that antique PLV, unless he really did steal it . . . Could he be a criminal? I don't know anything about him. The ad doesn't even give his name, or any way to contact him.

I twist onto my stomach. My jacket wraps tight. Wiggling it loose, I reach into the pocket for those insignias. TE. Probably some rinky-dink shipping line running ore from the colonies. Who else would hire a bum like him?

But pilot's wings are pilot's wings . . .

No. It's hopeless. I'm never going on a Moon mission with that old spacer. Pilots don't drink. Pilots can't be crippled, either. I'll never find out why the cabin boy has to be short. Never learn more about the Counselors.

Still in search mode, the computer screen glows patiently from across the room. That can't be true, what he said about them being able to make you forget. The booze must have fogged his brain.

But you know, I've never searched "Counselor" before.

I glance at my open bedroom door. Listen. Mark's not home yet. With a push off the bed, I go close the door. Rest my back against it. Hesitate, suddenly nerved up. Like I'm about to do something wrong. Why should I feel guilty about wanting to search that topic?

My mouth is dry. I work my tongue around to get up a little spit, loosen the words. "Search Counselor."

Entries fill the screen as I walk back toward the desk. I've picked up enough of the jargon after six years of sessions to recognize a promising listing: TREATMENT OPTIONS.

Sweat tingles across my forehead. Maybe because I haven't even taken my jacket off yet. I shrug out of it, touch the entry. Another big, long list.

One stands out: MNEMONIC SUPPRESSION.

Mnemonic. I remember that word from helping Mark with some artificial intelligence programming.

It's Greek. Means something like memory tricks, things like "*i* before *e* except after *c*."

I reach for the screen, but a hunger pang stops me. Should've had a snack. Can't stop for a snack now. Reach again, but my stomach clenches once more. It's not hunger. More like how my insides shrink watching the NewsVid, just before the image of the crashing shuttle appears.

Weird.

I force my whole body to bow toward the computer until my outstretched finger touches the screen over MNEMONIC SUPPRESSION.

THIS PAGE CANNOT BE DISPLAYED
YOUR SOFTWARE NEEDS UPDATING

Now that's really weird. Mark never lets our software get out of date. I try a different URL, hoping to find a cross-link back to mnemonic suppression. The few links that I do find all lead back to the same dead end. Just my luck today. A chance to go to the Moon with a drunk. And no answers about the Counselor the first time I ever think to look.

At least I don't feel sick anymore. It must have just been a hunger pang, like I thought. Better get a snack and tackle that science project.

Before heading for the kitchen, I reach under the bed and haul out my Val Thorsten Jupiter Mission footlocker. Open it. Sitting on top is a Pilot Achievement Award folder with an official fan club certificate and replica medal inside. There's a blank space for your name on the certificate. Mine's still blank. I've vowed not to write my name in until I can do AstroNav.

Scooping up the old spacer's insignias from the bed, I drop them in and slam down the lid. Bum that he is, he's light-years ahead of me. Without AstroNav, nobody would even hire me to run ore.

By the time Mark gets home, I'm well into my science project. He sails through the front door and into the living room pushing waves of cheeriness. He must have had a good date. Things are sure going fine for *him* with Dad gone. "Hey, hi, Stub."

"Don't call me that!"

"Touchy." Mark shrugs off his pack and drops it. "Hey, is that the RugBot?"

"Yeah." Pieces of it and tools and the rest of my science project are spread all around me on the carpet.

"The bread maker, too?!"

"Shhh." I'm trying to pull the stair-climbing gear from the RugBot. It's perfect for the crank of my mechanoid jack-in-the-box creation. But the gear is in a position where I have to use my right hand to hold the pliers. The scar across my palm starts cramping just as I get a grip on the gear. I lose my hold. The pliers drop down into the RugBot's housing.

"Shoot." I shake the stiffness out of my hand. I don't care about the ugly scar, but I worry there might be some lingering nerve damage that'll make piloting hard. I don't even remember burning it—Dad says it happened when I was little, an accident with a laser in his lab—but it sure seems the damage should have healed completely by now.

The old spacer's voice comes into my head. *They can make you forget.*

I wish I could forget he ever said that! The alcohol had a good grip on him by then. I bet it's just spacer superstition. I was too *young* to remember, that's all.

Ignoring the ache and the spacer's nonsense, I snag the pliers and take another stab at the gear.

Mark squats at the edge of the construction zone. "What *are* you doing?"

"Making an electrodigital jack-in-the-box. Watch." I set the bread maker timer for five seconds and press *start*. The motor whirs and the little shaft waiting for a crank spins. Zero. The top flies open. Four feet of slinky toy leaps for the ceiling. Mark falls back onto his rump. "Neat, huh?"

"Where's Jack? And will it ever make bread again?"

"I'm gonna put a rocket on it."

"What else?" Mark rolls his eyes.

I shove the RugBot under his nose. "Can *you* see a lock pin in there?"

"Give it a rest." He stands up. Unzips his Hawk's team jacket halfway. "Look what came in the mail."

He fishes out a flat packet about the size of a notebook. It's wrapped in thermax. Only things from space come in thermax.

I make for it like a gravitron missile. "What is it?"

"Don't know." Mark holds it up out of reach. "Might be a birthday cake, with ice cream—freeze-dried, for little spacemen!"

He thumps me on the head, full of his own joke. I jump. Grab for it. But can't win against his height. "Give it to me, monkey arms!"

"Don't get sore. Here." One great thing about Mark—he's got pimples, a girlfriend, and smelly sweat socks, but he's not a jerk about important stuff.

"It's from Dad!" The package is flexible and lightweight. I turn it over and over. No rattles. No sloshes.

"Thermax blocks X-ray vision," Mark says.

I peel open the thermax, revealing black gift wrap, dotted with silver Milky Way spirals. There's a thumb-sized bump in the middle. A 3-Vid. I rip off the paper.

"Oh wow! Solar Time Warp! This isn't due out until next month. How'd Dad get a copy?"

"Note on the back."

I turn it over.

An early present, Stewart!

Waiting for the Moon run on Olympus Space Station, I met a pilot bringing a shipment of these in from the asteroid belt. I bribed him MUCHO to give me a copy. You'll be the first kid on Earth to see Val Thorsten's latest adventure!

Had quite a talk with this pilot. Believe me, you're better off with your dreams of Val Thorsten than you'd ever be with the reality of a six-month ore run to Jupiter.

We'll talk more when I get home.

Love you both,

Dad.

"I'm not going to run ore!" I fling the gift away and drop onto the couch, jouncing the springs as hard as I can. I'm going to be the next Val Thorsten. But Dad doesn't understand.

Mom would have.

A picture of her hangs on the wall across from me. I really, really hate that picture, but it's the only one Dad will put up. Nothing's wrong with *Mom*. She's short like me, and beautiful. Her eyes are like cat's eyes, wide open and intense. Her curly brown hair frames her impish features. That's how they describe her in NewsVids and articles: impish. I hate the picture because she's wearing a dress. In my favorite pictures of her, she's always in a flight suit.

"Why isn't Dad *proud* I want to be like Mom?"

Mark looks down at me with sad eyes. Then they go unfocused. He's reaching back, back for memories of Mom. He's so lucky to *have* memories, even if they hurt. *Bitter fruit.* That's what the old spacer called bad memories. I feel guilty not telling Mark about him. But with messages like that from Dad, I've got to keep my options open.

"Having a rocket pilot in the family isn't all that fun," Mark finally says. "She was . . . gone . . . a lot."

"*Of course* she was gone. The shortest time to Mars is two months."

"And you would've been right out there with her." Mark drops onto the opposite end of the couch. "You'll make it. Know why? Because you're like me and we're both like Mom—stubborn. I'm going to be a cryptographer and marry Andrea. You're going to fly rockets. In the long run, Dad will have to accept that."

"Stubborn isn't good enough. I mean, toughing it out will work for you. You've got time. Not me. I'm thirteen *tomorrow*. You have to pass the exam for

Space Academy while you're thirteen years old. If Dad doesn't change his mind and let me go to camp this session, I won't have a chance of passing."

Mark shakes his head, says what he always says when I remind him of the details. "That's such a stupid system."

"Well, it's the way it is and Dad knows it. He knows I have to be able to do AstroNav to pass. It's almost like he *wants* me to fail."

"It's not like that."

"What *is* it like then?" I tuck up onto my knees to face him at the other end of the couch. "Why won't he let me go?"

"I hate this!" Mark explodes to his feet. "Dad should be here. He should talk to you! I can't do it!"

He kicks the RugBot. Its plastic shell shatters against the wall. He stands rigid for a heartbeat, then picks up the largest piece. He cradles it like a dead bird.

"I broke it."

"Don't worry, it'll be easier to get the gear out." He was supposed to laugh, but he just stands there staring at it. Makes me nervous. "Hey, should I call the Counselor?"

"No." Mark tosses the RugBot onto the parts pile. "Listen. How'd you like another early present? Wait right there until I call you."

Mark heads for the workroom before I can protest. He's not fooling me. He knows something about why Dad doesn't want me to become a pilot. And I know he'll never tell. We *are* both like Mom—stubborn.

Mark calls and I'm moving off the couch, too curious to sulk. The workroom is blazing with a bright, clean light. The source is a three-foot-diameter Moon floating in the holochamber at the center of the room. The hologram projection looks so real I feel the pull of gravity! It's a piece of cake to pick out Copernicus Crater. But even at this magnification, Luna Base isn't visible.

"Happy birthday." Mark's at the computer console on the other side of the room. His face glows red from the tactical display screen he uses when hacking.

"Wow! Where'd you get such a great holodisc?"

"It's not a disc. That's live from a HOOPscope."

"A HOOPscope! You hacked their system?" I circle around the holochamber and walk over to the computer console. Mark is wearing this big, self-satisfied grin. He ought to be! HOOPscope stands for High Orbit Observation Platform telescope. They're the most powerful eyes in the solar system. Astronomers fight like dogs to get time on them.

"Hard job," Mark says. "Been at it for weeks. Besides getting around TIA, they've got some awesome security algorithms of their own I had to crack. People that sharp might be fun to work for someday."

Mark's really taken a risk to get this. The Total Information Awareness security system is supposed to protect the entire network from terrorists and spies and hackers. "Good luck! If they ever find out you broke in—"

"They won't," Mark says with typical hacker bravado. "What do you want to see?"

I know exactly what I want to see. "Can I do it myself?"

"Well . . ." Mark hates how clumsy I am with new software.

"I thought this was *my* present?"

"Sure." Mark calls up the help menu. The Moon disappears, leaving only a feeble redness around us. It makes the room feel small and secret, like a submarine. And that seems right because we're doing something wrong.

I sit at the console. Mark settles on the couch behind me. He pops a *Hacker* magazine capsule into his FlexyPad. He knows this is going to take awhile. Mark's a fish in water when it comes to software. I'm more like a boat on a search and destroy mission; thorough, but plodding. Before long, Mark is clicking impatiently through the pages of the magazine.

At last the monitor flashes: COORDINATES? I know the numbers by heart: 128 321 004 range sphere M. The three-foot Moon comes back, bright as a bolt of lightning.

I toggle the joystick. Faster than any spaceship, we zoom in on the surface. A blur of mountains, crags, harsh shadows, and dazzling light flicker within the chamber. I glimpse red, white, and blue. Release the joystick. The United States flag fills the holochamber. Smack on target: Tranquility Base, where the first men landed on the Moon.

"I should've guessed." Mark steps up behind me.

The flag stands tall, the cloth frozen in a timeless ripple. It's the only real flag left from all the Moon missions. The ultraviolet light of the sun destroyed the others. This one survived because the rocket exhaust from the *Eagle*'s liftoff knocked it over and covered it with a protective layer of dust. Now it's safely sealed within UV blocking film. There was quite a controversy about whether to leave it in the dust or restore it when the site became a Humanity Park. I'm glad it's up: Those heroes deserve it that way.

I toggle back.

The base of the Lunar Excursion Module comes into view. Life-support packs, overshoes, and other junk lie in the dust at the bottom of the ladder— deadweight Neil Armstrong and Buzz Aldrin threw out of the ascent stage to make room for moon rocks. I zoom in on the surface near a landing pad. A footprint fills the holochamber.

"Maybe that's the *first* step." I lean over the console and reach into the perfect image, expecting to feel moon dust in the powdery tread marks.

"Give me a break! Those guys walked all over that site!"

I pan the area, tracking the footsteps I've dreamed of walking in. The fence surrounding Tranquility Base comes into view. It's a tourist barrier, to make sure this site remains undisturbed forever.

"Someday, I'm going there."

"Nobody *wants* to go to the Moon."

Mark's right. All the action is in the asteroid belt, on Mars, and on the moons of Jupiter. People left our Moon behind a long time ago, at least the light side of it. They had to. There were so many strip mines and bases and solar power plants that people on Earth noticed the changes. All the nations agreed this was a bad thing. The light side was declared off limits to more development.

Mark says, "Let's practice some AstroNav before they bump us. The HOOPscope has a gold-class training program. Maybe it'll be as good as the one at camp. We can find that star you love, you know, the squashed bug."

"Betelgeuse? I don't know . . ."

"Come on, you're always saying I don't help enough."

He's got me there. "Okay, call it up."

He reaches over me to activate the program. It turns out to be pretty similar to the one I use with the CompTeach. But without that electronic buddy prompting me through the tough parts, the calculations to lock onto Betelgeuse become a torture. A dozen tries and the last few steps still won't gel.

"I can't *do* AstroNav!"

"I think you're right, Stub. Punch autofind. Maybe we can see where you went wrong."

I stab the key. Instantly, the image of the star Betelgeuse fills the holochamber like a million silver needles frozen in a crystal ball. Mark runs his fingers down the comparative columns on the display. "Huh. You've got everything right."

"I always get the *pieces* right. But then it's like I have astro-dyslexia or something."

A warning alarm sounds, loud and shrill. Not much different than the whine in my voice a moment ago.

"Feely!" Mark pushes me aside. Feelies are bad news. They're software spiders TIA sends out to track down hackers. The alarm means one is nibbling on Mark's data stream.

Of course, he's ready for this and starts slapping down toggles, dumping his preloaded Crumbeaters into the link. Like in the fairy tale, they'll sweep away his cybertrail, wipe out any memory of his hack in the vast network that sprawls all the way to Jupiter.

I stare at the back of my brother's head as he works his disappearing act. Mark's brilliant enough to outwit TIA, the most sophisticated intelligence gathering system in the solar system. He would never let our software get out of date.

The sick-to-my-stomach feeling I had when searching "Counselor" comes back. What if that dead end wasn't just bad luck? What if the Counselor is monitoring my computer? It might not want me to learn anything about mnemonic suppression.

Maybe the old spacer wasn't talking nonsense after all. Maybe he really does know some of their secrets.

Two days ago my biggest problem was trying to convince Dad to send me to camp. Now I feel like there's this hidden dimension around me—a parallel universe. In that world, something is wrong with me. It's shaping the way Dad and Mark and the Counselor are acting. Maybe it's ruining my chances of becoming a pilot.

"All right!" Mark hits a final switch and rolls his

chair away from the console. He spins in it, tri-umphant. "Another nanosecond escape."

"Listen, Mark. I have to see the Counselor again."

Mark jerks to a stop, looks at me sharp. "That's funny. A message came in while we were busy. First thing tomorrow, the Counselor wants to see you."

4

MISSION TIME

T minus 03:21:04

WHEN it begins, I don't even realize I'm in a version of the box dream. There's a choking whiteness all around me that stinks of chemicals—crash foam! With a kind of running breaststroke, I move through it. The foam thins. Becomes a fizzing stream at my feet and . . . there's the black shoe box.

The tiny red door is ajar. The foam bubbles out of it. I glimpse a row of seats, upside down; somebody is in one of them, looking out, and I feel this urgent need to talk to him.

But the old spacer picks up the box. The door swings shut. Hatred surges in me and I yell, "Give it to me, monkey arms!"

He laughs. A bubble of alcohol breath engulfs me. I grab for the door handle—suddenly normal size. Heat like acid splashes across my palm.

I recoil, fall . . .

spacer and box rocket away in an explosion
and fall and fall until I strain through the weave of
cotton sheets to land back in myself in my bed.

Wake up.

I clutch my right hand to my chest. Curl my body
protectively around it. Feels like a new burn cuts
across my palm. I bury my face in the pillow. Groan
out the pain.

Can't let Mark hear.

He'll tell the Counselor.

The old scar throbs, forcing short breaths. I don't
dare look. Afraid I'll find the palm burned red
and raw.

Sweat soaks the pillowcase. I press my burning
hand against the moist coolness of the cloth. Ahhh . . .
I lay my cheek over my hand. Try to take regular
breaths. Draw into a tighter ball beneath the covers.

I am Stewart Edward Hale. I'm four feet three and
nine sixteenth inches tall. Short, like Mom. Margaret
Jane Hale. Maggie to fellow spacers.

My birthday is October 28. Today. In the year 2165.
I'm thirteen.

I live in the Singleton Apartments, New Canaveral,
Florida, with my older brother, Mark, and my father,
Theodore Vincent Hale, Ted. Before, we lived in New
Frisco, California, in a house.

There was an orchard
and a tree
and a toy ship . . .

Even under the covers, I sense the change as a squiggly comes on, then the darkness explodes with light . . .

I'm on the kitchen floor in the bright California sunshine; playing with my Lance Ramjet and watching Mom's legs flash by me.

Back and forth. Pantry . . . counter . . . fridge . . . stove.

She's mixing up blueberry waffles.

Special food for my special day.

"Oops . . ." Splat. An egg hits the floor, startling me out of my spaceship dreams.

Back under the sheets in the ordinary darkness of my bedroom, my lungs burn. I've been holding my breath. I gulp in fresh air, smell the yeasty smell of home-made blueberry waffles.

"Mom?" I fight out from under the covers. *"Mom!"*

I run for the kitchen, pull up short in the doorway. Mark is at the counter, his back to me. Mom's ancient waffle iron sits on the table, steaming. It's shaped like a flying saucer, a squat, round massiveness balanced on a pedestal. A family heirloom for over 150 years and a horrible energy waster. I didn't know we still had it. The morning sun sparkles off the silver surface.

The sparkles fracture into a rustle of green leaves . . .

The tree . . . an ancient, bent early snow apple, with the thick, forked limb sturdy enough to support a tree house.

"Stewart? You okay?"

"I'm . . . the smell . . . my spaceship tree house." A different birthday. A special present. "Who helped me build that?"

"Gosh, that was so long ago. We saved tinfoil for months to make the shiny skin. I'd almost forgotten that!"

"But who built it with me?"

"Mom did, of course." Mark takes a platter of waffles out of the warmer and sets them on the table. "Happy birthday!"

"How come I don't remember that?"

"You just did." Mark flips a couple waffles onto my plate. "Come on. They'll get cold."

I sit and butter them. Drizzle syrup into each little square. Eyes closed, I pretend the first bite is a PLV and slowly dock it in my mouth. I'm hoping something magic will happen—another memory. All I get is reminded that Mark's a great cook.

The disappointment makes me more determined than ever to get some answers from the Counselor.

First thing when I get to school, I drop off my science project, then head for the Counselor's office. The project's not my best effort. I could barely concentrate once I decided to confront the Counselor with what the old spacer told me. I wish I could've talked to him again, but I couldn't just run out on Mark's birthday breakfast, and then there was no time left for a detour.

I slip a hand into my pants pocket. Run my finger over the sharp corners of the Space Academy Camp application folded there.

No harm in dreaming.

As soon as I step into the Counselor's office—*bing*—the sign changes to "ENTER, PLEASE." No waiting today. I step up to the session room door. Hesitate with my thumb hovering over the latch plate. Draw in a deep, steadying breath. I am going to make it talk about what *I* want for once.

I mash my thumb against the latch plate. The door slides open. The huge screen on the wall behind the empty desk declares:

MRS. PHILLIPS REGRETS SHE CANNOT APPEAR IN PERSON,
STEWART. AUTOMATED SIMULATION IS DOWNLOADING.

When I sit on the stool in front of the desk, the holofield glitters, filling the chair with Mrs. Phillips's image. Sensors whir behind the screen. The hologram leans toward me. "You have been in therapy for six years, Stewart. Suddenly you search for information about us. Why?"

A frozen moment, like when someone walks in on you in the bathroom. I was all ready for a fight and now the Counselor practically admits it was watching me. "So you *were* monitoring my computer yesterday."

"Yes. In certain special cases, TIA is authorized to inform us of your activities. If you have questions about us, you should ask them here."

"What about my rights? You can't just spy on me! Don't I have rights?"

"You *do* have rights, Stewart, but they are slightly reduced in special cases. Don't worry." The image smiles. "The information is used only to assist with your therapy."

"What's special about my case?"

"Parental permission is required for me to answer that question." The image folds its hands together. "There are many things we can speak of without your father's permission, Stewart. Please, ask your questions."

"Did you make me forget things?"

"Why would you think we had done that?"

"Because I forget too many things I *should* remember, like how Mom and I built my spaceship tree house. How could an important memory like that just be gone?"

The image sits up straight. "When did you recall this?"

"This morning."

"You have withheld vital information." The little pointy place in the middle of the top lip gets sharper. "We are disappointed, Stewart."

"*I'm* disappointed! You didn't help me at all yesterday. It was a terrible session. The worst!"

"Is that why you went to the Old Spaceport afterward?"

"You tracked me?" Does it know about the old spacer?

"You feel closer to your mother there, don't you, Stewart?" The voice is soft, soothing, the nearest to the real Mrs. Phillips it ever gets. "Closer to your dream of spaceflight."

"There's this fence. That's what I feel, this fence between me and everything I want."

"Did the pilot promise to help you?"

"Pilot? What pilot?" If TIA has identified him, then he wasn't lying to me about being a real pilot.

"This pilot, Stewart." The screen flashes a head shot of the old spacer. Enough background shows to let me know he's sleeping on the bench at Gamma Station. Is that *now*? Or yesterday? Will *I* come into the picture next?

"Did he tell you his name?"

Not a statement. A question. It has pictures, but no audio. It doesn't know what we talked about—doesn't know I planned to meet him again. I cling to that. Shake my head, no.

"Voice response required."

"No." The sensors focus—to check if I'm lying! Why is his name so important?

"Did you tell him *your* name?"

"No."

"We are glad you have that much sense, Stewart. You should not be alone with strange men in deserted TransHubs. You will avoid this man in the future."

"Why?"

"You will avoid this man."

"Because he told the truth? Is that why?"

"You will—"

I jump up. Slam my hands down on the desk. "Why did I forget about the tree house?!"

The image freezes, then fractures into a thousand cubical elements. I stare through the suddenly faceted eyes to whatever sensor array is behind the screen.

"You're a machine. You must answer!"

"It is essential to maintain trust." The mouth doesn't move. The voice becomes mechanical. "This is a critical time for you, Stewart. Perhaps we should review past events."

The overhead lights go out. The screen flickers. The pale blue sky from the opening scene of the NewsVid washes through the frozen hologram.

"No!" I back away, smack into the stool. "Don't show that!"

"This has helped. It *will* help." The cubes meld. The image regains structure and reclaims Mrs. Phillips's voice. "Watch, please."

"I won't!"

The volume cranks. The splutter of static is like a cymbal crash next to my ears. Tower Control booms, "Contact lost with incoming."

I bolt for the door. Mash my thumb against the latch plate.

Locked!

"Let me out!" Kick it! Pound it!

The NewsVid sound mutes.

"Stewart, please calm yourself."

"Let me out!"

"Stewart, return to the stool. Focus on the screen."

"No!"

"Alert! Alert!" The Counselor slips into its machine voice, blaring out the words. "Mrs. Phillips, report to session room immediately. Subject at serious risk of associative bifurcation."

"I'm not an experiment!"

"You must cooperate. Mrs. Phillips may not arrive quickly enough to prevent harm."

"Harm?! What's the matter with me?"

"Emergency conditions." The NewsVid freezes on the image of the upside-down shuttle. The scene strobes, seizes my gaze. I can't look away. "Stewart. Sit. Down. Now."

"NO!"

I grab the edge of the stool. Swipe it through the hologram. Spin around from not connecting with anything solid. Raising the stool over my head, I hurl it at the screen behind the desk. The screen implodes in a riot of short circuits, leaving the room barely lit with the glow from the hologram.

The soundtrack starts running again. The sound waves hit me with force, as if the Counselor lashed out with a fist.

"Stop!"

I clamp my hands over my ears. Stagger into the far

corner. The sound of the plunging shuttle bores through my hands.

I slide down to the floor.

The volume increases, ragged at the limits of the speaker's audio range. Scenes come, vivid on the inside of my squeezed-tight eyelids, as if the Newsvid is running in my brain. I slam my head against the wall. Pain blooms on my cheek, around my eye, weakens the images in my head.

Do it again.

Lights dance in my head.

Again!

The door opens.

"Ohmygod!" Mrs. Phillips staggers under the blast of sound. She shouts at her own hologram, almost invisible in the shaft of light from the waiting room. "What are you doing?"

The image screeches back, "Necessary treatment."

"Stop!" She rushes to the desk, nose to nose with the wavering image. "Stop at once!"

"Necessary—"

"Override! Code seven, triangle, beta!"

The hologram disappears. The soundtrack goes silent.

"Stewart? Stewart, where are you?"

Mrs. Phillips looks anxiously around the room. But

she's caught in the glare from the open door and can't see me. She shields her eyes. The light glints on a hypodermic needle in her hand.

"Stewart? Can you answer me?"

Blindly, she steps my way.

I take her down with a scissors kick.

She sprawls onto the floor. The arm holding the hypo folds against her stomach and hisses out its supply of tranquilizer.

"Oh no . . . no . . ." she groans, reaching toward me. "Don't run—"

Then her eyes turn up white as the tranquilizer takes hold.

5

MISSION TIME

T minus 00:45:05

THE old spacer's asleep on the bench, just like in the picture the Counselor showed me.

"Wake up." Barely a whisper. Cameras? Mikes? I'm glancing around, but I'd never see them anyway. "Mister! Wake up!"

One eye opens, rakes me head to toe.

"Beat it. I'm waiting for a midget."

The eye closes.

"No! You don't understand—I'm in trouble!" I shove his bulk.

Snake quick, his hand darts from the folds of his jacket and grabs my wrist. His reflexes are better than mine!

"Don't do that again."

I try to yank away.

His grip tightens. He draws me close. "Sweet Neptune, what happened to your face?"

"My face?" I remember banging the side of my head against the wall. I touch my cheek. Pain flares. "We've got to get out of here! They'll see us soon as she wakes up!"

"What *are* you talking about?" He releases his grip. With a grunt and a curse, he sits up.

"I smashed the Counselor."

"With your head, right?"

"No, a stool. It tried to brainwash me. Even smashed . . . it wouldn't stop. Then Mrs. Phillips came in. She had a needle! I knocked her down and she injected herself. I don't know how long she'll be out. Get up, will you! Before they come after us!"

"Us?"

"They had your picture. Sleeping right here!"

He looks over my head into corners, then drops his gaze to confront me with narrowed eyes. "What have you mixed me up in? Huh?"

"I had to find out if it was goofing up my AstroNav. It told me to stay away from you. It wanted me to watch Mom's crash all over again. Tried to push it into my head." I can still feel the hard walls trapping me in the corner, see the glint of light on that needle . . .

"I don't need this." He looks away.

"It's your fault. You're the one who said they can

make you forget. All I did was ask it to tell the truth. It went haywire! You have to help me!"

"Have to? Like fate, huh?" He laughs, a dry, tight sound.

"Please . . ." My teeth chatter. I notice the chill air for the first time. Running off, I forgot my jacket.

"Sit down."

"No! We've got to go away from here!"

"It isn't easy to hide from TIA, kid. Gotta think, so sit down." He slaps the bench.

He's going to help me! My knees fold from relief and I collapse onto the seat next to him. He knows what we're up against. Maybe he can come up with a plan.

He shrugs out of his jacket, wincing as he draws his arms from the sleeves. He wraps it around me. It settles heavy on my shoulders. The pockets must be crammed with stuff. Smells a little sour, but it's sleep-hot. I pull my legs into the cave of it, too.

"Have a sip of this." He takes a squeeze bottle out of his pants pocket. He folds my fingers around it, urges them toward my mouth. "Do it. I've seen shock plenty of times, kid, and that's where you're headed."

Dad's let me sip wine before, but this stuff grabs your attention in a whole different way.

"Hey, that's enough!" He snatches it back, fires in a mouthful for himself. "When did this happen?"

"Fifteen minutes ago? Longer since we've been talking."

He looks at the Chronomatrix on his wrist. His lips draw thin and straight.

"Go buy a soda. Machine's right there." He points to a cluster of vending machines along the same wall the bench is against.

He's crazy! "We can't sit here drinking soda!"

"Not to drink. For that bruise on your cheek. Gotta get something cold on it to stop the swelling."

I pull the jacket tight and head for the soda machine, press my thumb to the charge plate.

TIA can trace that.

I never worried about TIA before. Mark knows a lot . . .

Mark! Has anyone told him yet? Does anyone know anything yet? Or is Mrs. Phillips still zonked out?

She shut the Counselor down. Maybe she was going to help me. I just ran away. What if she's hurt? I just ran.

Two Helium Zingers drop out of the slot. I might drink one. Supposed to be good for queasy stomachs. When I come back to the bench, he sits rigid as a block of ice, staring out at the ships on their launch-pads.

"Tend to that bruise." He doesn't even glance at me. "And keep your mouth shut."

Gingerly, I press the cold, sweating can to my right cheek. Hiss in a sharp breath. But the cold feels good. Slowly, I rotate the can.

"Okay." He lurches to his feet with a curse and a grab at the small of his back. "Come on."

He bends down only far enough to catch the strap of the duffel bag. He hitches the strap over his shoulder, then, Igor-like, limps toward the rear of the station. I stand up, but it's tricky holding the sodas and keeping the jacket from falling off. He's around the corner already. I rush to catch up.

He's standing behind some kind of wheeled thing.

"What's the matter?" He shrugs the duffel into the back of the thing. "Haven't you ever seen a golf cart before?"

"Not with *wheels*!"

"Get in." He hitches up his right leg and works it over the sidewall into the driver's side. The cart tips as he shifts all his weight onto that foot and hauls the rest of his body in using the steering wheel.

"Where are we going?"

He gestures toward the ocean and now I see that the cart is parked at the beginning of the long road out to Pad 12—must be at least a mile. The ancient concrete is heaved and shattered, but there's a smooth path of fresh sand down the middle of the decayed roadway. Two ruts are packed hard from frequent trips. His berth. He's been living out there with the rocket! Probably cleared away any surveillance stuff. But he's wrong if he thinks Pad 12 is a safe place to hide.

"It won't work. Your ad is on my computer. They'll know where I am."

He turns the key. "We'll be gone before anyone comes."

"Gone . . . ?" I look toward Pad 12. One old PLV, operational. He *does* have a plan. To blast off. With me. Now.

"Take off that wrist yapper."

I shield the wireless OmniLink on my wrist with a soda. "I can't just *disappear!*"

"That's sort of the point, kid."

"I have to call Mark."

"Not with that. Easy to spot as a supernova."

"But—"

"We'll call him from orbit. Safer that way."

Orbit. He really means it.

"Ditch it and get in. We've got to keep moving now."

Suddenly, he's the one in a hurry. I pull my gaze from the rocket, toss the sodas onto the seat. Hooking a finger under the stretch band of the OmniLink, I slip it off. The breeze slides coldly over the bone-white skin of my naked wrist. That skin only sees daylight during a bath. There aren't even any little hairs growing there anymore. We were always told: Never be without your OmniLink. Never talk to strangers.

I look at the TransTube curving away from the station toward the city. Things don't seem that simple anymore.

"Don't fool yourself, kid. You were lucky today. They won't screw up again."

I drop the OmniLink into the sand and hop in.

He lays the throttle to the floor. Sand sprays, tires squeal, then catch, bucking us into motion. I slam back against the seat. The soda cans go flying out of my hands. No acceleration dampers; this sure isn't an ordinary golf cart! Even the modern air-riders don't go this fast.

I whoop and shout against the breeze. "What did you *do* to this thing?"

The corner of his mouth curls up a bit. "Double wired the traction pack."

Bad news for the motor. Then it dawns on me. Nobody's going to drive this cart away from the gantry. It'll be burned toast as soon as we . . . blast off.

We're close enough now to get a good look at the rocket. Not a fleck of paint left on it. The skin is as rusty brown as an uscrubbed potato. Black stains fan down the sides from each of the staging joints. I know my boosters. This is an old ICBM. A lot of nuclear missiles were converted to PLVs during the worldwide disarmament a half century ago. They were a quick, cheap, and dirty way to orbit for people who couldn't afford a ride on shuttles.

Not exactly what I imagined making my first trip to space in.

Taller and taller it looms until even with my head tilted way back, I can't see it all at once. We coast to a stop right under the rocket nozzles.

A smell of burned motor wiring wafts up from below my seat. I hop out and step away from the cart, worried it might burst into flames. He's either not worried or can't move any faster, I'm not sure which.

We've pulled up next to a tent. A tidy campsite is arranged compactly around it. The PLV towers silently above us. The only sound comes from the waves breaking on the beach just over the sand dunes.

"Grab that duffel." He heads for the open mesh-wire elevator at the base of the gantry.

Guess he doesn't need anything from his camp.

I sling the duffel over my shoulder. It isn't too heavy, but you'd never guess that from the way it bent him over. Whatever is inside shifts around like potatoes in a sack, settling into a lumpy bulge at the bottom.

I hustle into the cage. He pulls the door closed. It

clatters like a freight train. The elevator lurches upward so fast my knees nearly buckle. I like that feeling.

The sound of the breakers fades as the elevator lifts us out of the deep shadow between the tail fins. A light wind blows; the air coming off the sun-drenched beach is warmer here.

The rocket is only a few feet away. On this side, the ocean side, it's in even worse shape. The salt spray has left pits in the metal. The black stains glisten wetly. The hair rises at the back of my neck.

"Is this really okay to fly?"

"I've checked this little Roman candle out nozzles to nose cone, kid. She's sound enough."

The elevator stops. A walkway leads to the capsule hatch, which isn't much bigger than a manhole cover. Can he even fit through that?

"I'll take my jacket back now."

It's chilly up here. Goose bumps rise immediately on my arms. He doesn't put the jacket on, but walks ahead, punches a few commands on the latch plate. The hatch pops open, revealing two reclining flight seats crammed in a hollow ball barely the size of a refrigerator.

"You first."

Halfway across the walkway, I stop. I look through the steel grating under my feet, down the long, rusty body of the rocket to the hard, hard ground, 150 feet below. The failure rate for these things is a bit higher than the rocket Dad went up in.

"You with me, kid, or what?"

"Yeah." I crawl through the tiny hatch.

I'm going to be in so much trouble!

6

MISSION TIME

T minus 00:06:06

IT'S super cramped inside the capsule, but warm.

With one knee resting on each seat back, I try to straighten up. The padding is so spongy it's hard to balance. Control knobs jab my head. I flop onto my back, sliding my legs under the instrument console at the same time. My toes aim toward the sky, but I can't see it. A launch shield covers the nose window.

The bare-bones instrument panel is dark. No power. How long will it take to bring this rocket online from cold shutdown?

Suddenly, the sunlight from the hatch goes out and I'm sitting in darkness.

"Hey!" I grope toward a dim halo of light around the hatch. My fingers find the rough canvas of the duffel.

The old spacer's voice comes muted. "Pull it in."

I pull. He pushes. The thing oozes in on top of me. In the struggle to wrestle it behind the seats, my 3-Vid goggles catch on something. They pop off the belt clip and clatter down behind the seats, just as the bag drops, too. Probably crushed them.

The jacket next. Down behind the seats.

The sunlight goes again. His head rams my arm.

"Scoot over."

I wiggle up against the curve of the cold metal wall. He squirms and grunts and twists until he flops into the seat nearest the hatch. He takes a deep breath, then hits a button on the control panel. The rocket shudders awake with a cascade of noises, like a truckload of empty tin cans pouring down through its innards.

T minus 60 flashes in bold digits on the countdown clock.

The hatch slams shut. The locks click. Interior lights soak us in red. He reaches across me and pulls the harness into place, snugs it tight. Once his own harness is on, he starts flipping switches. His left elbow jabs me with every move.

The numbers start dropping—*by the second!*

I thought we had at least an hour of preflight checks!

T minus 40.

This thing is already primed for blastoff.

T minus 30.

The fuel pumps grind up to speed, shivering the rocket from nozzles to nose cone.

T minus 15.

"Wait a minute! Who *are* you? Why do you need a *midget*?"

3—With a little smile

2—he puts his thumb over the

1—ignition button and

0—presses it.

The rocket motors erupt.

The initial jolt hits like a belly flop. The seat pads sigh and absorb me as the crushing, squeezing force of liftoff builds. The padding yields more, bulges around and over me. It's like sinking into chocolate pudding. My body shakes and quivers in its grip, chafing against the material.

In a few seconds, we hit maximum acceleration: ten g's. My weight goes from ninety pounds to nine hundred. Feels like an elephant is doing a slow roll over me. My chest collapses, leaving no room for air. I pull breaths, panting quick and shallow like a frightened chipmunk. My eyes wander out of sync and for a moment, I'm seeing both the old spacer on my right and a wildly vibrating strut on my left. Then blackness floods up to take away all sight.

I know the max-g boost phase will only last two

minutes, but time doesn't move in ordinary seconds under this kind of stress. I almost wish I'd pass out.

The rocket bucks. Stage one jettison. Acceleration eases back to a couple g's. I can see. I can breathe. I can handle six more minutes of this until we make orbit.

As the near senselessness caused by the boost phase wears off, the scar across my right palm starts to hurt. Figuring it's squashed in a fold of seat padding, I make a fist to protect the scar. The pain turns searingly hot, as if the rocket exhaust itself is flaring through my clenched fist. It burns like in the dream, but there's no pulling away. No waking up!

I was wrong. I won't make it. I'm going to scream.

Can't disgrace myself like that.

I think of Val in Venus: Inferno Below the Clouds; the steely control, the indifference to danger . . .

Another buck.

Fresh fire seems to flow through my palm.

I scream.

The last stage flames out.

The abrupt release of force kicks me against the harness, knocks my breath away, frees my arms. They swing up, reach the top of their arc. Instead of falling back into my lap, they hang in the air, floating.

Weightless!

We're in orbit. I stare at my palm hanging in the air

in front of my nose. The pain is gone, switched off with the rockets, leaving only a lingering pins and needles feeling. Seems impossible that it hurt so much just a moment ago.

"No more screaming. Understood?"

Startled, I pull my arms out of the air, too embarrassed to answer him.

With a gunshot-like pop, the launch shield ejects. A blue-white light whops my eyes, totally knocking me out of myself. The most beautiful view in the universe—Earth from orbit—blooms below us. We're pointed straight down at the ocean. Intense aquamarine, streaked with wispy clouds, fills the entire view port. Even though we're moving nearly eighteen thousand miles per hour, there's no sense of motion. The launch shield falls, winking sunlight as it tumbles toward burn up.

There's nothing left of the PLV except this tiny capsule. It isn't designed for any long duration flying, so he's got to get us docked to a ship or a space station soon. If we really are going to the Moon, there'll be a ship, somewhere close along this same orbit.

He fires a maneuvering thruster. The capsule tilts. The sky all drains to my side of the window, like when you flip one of those toys filled with different-colored sand. The upper atmosphere is pale blue, marbled with clouds. A vibrant band of neon blue marks where the edge of the world meets jet-black space. The shallow arc of the curve tells me we're in a low orbit.

An object appears ahead of us, a fiercely bright speck of white at first, quickly gaining in definition, becoming a triangular shape with an elongated nose. It looks like a badly designed paper airplane—body too fat, wings too small and far back—it's an old-fashioned space shuttle!

It hangs in orbit like a still life, crisp in every unbelievable detail. We're coming at it from "above." A cargo canister the size of our living room and two round propellant tanks crowd the cargo bay. But the cargo doors are gone, ripped away. Big areas on the hull show dull metal where hundreds of heat shield tiles are missing. There are *holes* in the wings!

"It's—it's—*space junk!*"

"Settle down. I've got to concentrate on docking."

"We can't go to the Moon in *that!*" Only one explanation makes sense. "It's a decoy, right? Like in Asteroid Run?"

"Sure, kid. Now shut up."

It *has* to be. Inside that blasted exterior is hidden some secret superduper drive system. And only *I* can help this guy test it. Except, he didn't want me. He was waiting for a midget . . .

A staccato blast of thrusters wrenches me back to reality.

Just behind the crew section is a combination docking adapter and air lock. It's shaped like an upside-down *T* with a big bulge at the intersection. That's the airlock chamber. The short legs stick out fore and aft from the air-lock chamber. One connects to the canister in the cargo bay; the other to the interior of the shuttle. The long leg of the *T* sticks out into space a few feet beyond the cockpit roof. A three-foot-diameter docking ring is on the end. Our target. It's an unusual arrangement, sticking out like that, but I guess it doesn't matter when there aren't any doors . . . jeez, it's a mess . . .

So is his flying!

Connecting up with that dock ought to be a routine maneuver. But he's in trouble. The thrusters are firing so often the capsule sounds like a steam engine at full throttle. He's breathing almost as fast. The sharp, sour odor of sweat fills the tiny space. His eyes shift from the docking radar to the view port. He jerks the joystick.

Bad move. Causes us to close in way too fast. The FlightComp flashes a warning. I knew it would. I've come to this point in simulations dozens of times—no bull's-eye for us. He has to pull out and try again.

But he doesn't.

The straps of my harness dig deep on impact. The air rings. The pod bounces off the dock. Sunshine flares inside for a moment. Then darkness. Tumbling. Falling out of orbit. We'll burn up!

"Do something!"

Sun again, lighting up his face. He's panicked. Locked up tight. I grab for a thruster.

"NO!" He smacks my hand away, connecting with the same knuckles I banged while watching Asteroid Run. It hurts! But at least I snapped him out of it.

He taps the keypad. Thrusters start popping off. The tumbling stops. He works the controls slowly, timidly, double-checking each move before triggering a thruster. Tense minutes pass this way until there's a solid thunk. The lock pins fire into place. He releases the joystick with a great blast of breath, followed by a ragged drag of air to refill his lungs. He sweeps the sheen of sweat from his forehead. Droplets float all around us.

"That was terrible! Even *I* can dock better than that!"

Did he hear me?

He coaxes a squeeze bottle out of a hip pocket, flips open the top, and pulls out the straw. His hands shake so badly, he almost can't get the straw between his lips. He sucks, grimacing like a nervous dog.

I must've been crazy, climbing into a rocket with him.

This is the Counselor's fault. What was it trying to do to me? When the screen strobed, I felt as if a leash jerked me up short. Like it was trying to control my brain. I *had* to escape.

But I don't have to stick with this guy. I can't. His flying's not going to improve the more he drinks.

He smacks his lips. The color is back in his face. The wide-open panic fades from his eyes. "You think you're better than me, huh, kid?"

"Yeah."

"That thruster"—he points the squeeze bottle at the one I almost fired—"would have blasted us straight out of orbit. So keep your hands off the controls."

"You should, too!"

He freezes for a second, then twists away, reaching to undo his harness buckle. The hatch cracks open with a gasp. The matching hatch on the docking ring opens. Sour air farts into the capsule.

With the flick of a finger against a panel edge, he sets his bulk in motion. He floats out of the seat and rotates in one fluid movement. He hooks the collar of his jacket, then corkscrews through the hatch in a headfirst glide into the air lock chamber.

He flows into the right-angle turn toward the lower deck of the crew section. He sure moves with a lot less trouble than on Earth—almost graceful. Can't say like a dolphin, not the way he looks, more like one of those manatees.

I hear a hatch clatter. Then another. Then his voice. "Bring that duffel when you come, kid."

My eyes fix on the joystick. It glistens, still moist with his sweat.

I can fly this thing. Just couldn't think very well with it tumbling before. I'll go to Olympus Space Station. Wait for Dad there. Safe from Counselors. Safe from this guy's flying.

I undo my harness so I can reach the hatch. I haul on the dock hatch first, but I'm the one who moves instead. My head slams into the rivets around the rim. What am I, the Universe's punching bag all of a sudden?

My own fault this time, though. You've got to do things different in zero-g. I hook my foot in a harness strap, pull again. The hatch swings closed.

I settle into the pilot's seat. Buckle up. Look at the controls. They're a kaleidoscope of confused colors. In simulators, there's a mission profile already in the FlightComp. I'm starting from scratch.

Calm down. Look for function blocks.

Okay, there's the FlightComp. I key in for undocking. A few panels come to life.

Now what?

The ship-to-ship intercom buzzes. "Cuttin' out?"

I jump, but he can't see that. "Thought I might."

Talking tough helps me feel tougher.

"Checked the thruster reserves yet?"

It takes a few seconds of searching even to *find* the fuel gauges. Inside the three small, round dials, the neon red needles rest hard to the left—empty!

His lousy flying used up all the fuel! Sweat blooms on my face. If I cut loose without fuel, the PLV would fall out of orbit. This tiny capsule isn't built to withstand reentry. I would've burned up.

Out the window, beyond the razor-straight edge of the shuttle's tail, beyond the geometrically perfect cone of the engine nozzles, the ragged west coast of Africa is a long, long way down.

"Toggle back into standby, kid. And don't forget the duffel."

MISSION TIME

T plus 00:31:07

THE tunnel leading from the docking ring to the airlock chamber is so narrow even *I* can't stand straight in it. Pushing the duffel through the hatch, I drop after it feetfirst. Grabbing a handhold, I stop inside the tunnel to close the capsule hatch, then the hatch on the docking ring. I drift into the airlock chamber, a cylinder twice as roomy as the capsule and reeking of mothballs.

The smell comes from a space suit lashed to the curving wall. Bulky, old style, and small. For someone under four feet five inches. A dinosaur compared to the suit Dad had, it's probably been in storage for the last fifty years, like everything else about the old spacer.

Why isn't there one for him? That's not safe, especially in a tub as old as this one. Leaks happen.

Anchoring my foot in a wall strap, I pull the airlock hatch into the docking tunnel closed. Two other narrow tunnels lead from the air lock, each a little longer than I am tall but both too narrow to stand up in. One goes into the shuttle. The other, sealed off by a closed hatch, connects to the enormous canister in the cargo bay. Through the air lock's hatch window, the bright blue handle of the canister's hatch catches my eye. I'm tempted to take a peek. Maybe it's a habitat or science module. Maybe I could find out what this mission is about. But then again, it could be full of mission support equipment in an airless can. Too risky.

Turning away from temptation, I snag the strap on the duffel and kick off into the tunnel leading to the crew section of the shuttle. There's a little backward tug as the duffel strap goes taut, then the bag sails into middeck with me. I'm closing fast on a wall covered with broken lockers. With no way to stop! I smack the wall, rebound into the oncoming duffel, and stop tangled with it in midair.

Action and reaction. I'm a living physics experiment!

One of those uncontrollable moronic grins takes over my face. Pretty quick, though, the look of the place sobers me up.

Middeck is about fourteen feet wide, ten long fore to aft, and eight tall deck to ceiling. The shower, toilet, and environmental control unit stick into the open space, creating odd angles. It feels roomy after the capsule, but it wouldn't feel that way with a crew of six living and working here.

The place shows signs of real heavy use: scratches, scuff marks, stains on everything. The privacy screen that should surround the toilet is missing. Dents and gouges mar the front panel of the environment control unit, like someone used a hammer on it. No wonder the air stinks.

This just gets worse and worse. After a moment's hesitation, I seal the air lock behind me. No escape that way.

The scar cramps as I turn the handle. I've overstressed my hand opening and closing so many hatches. They're everywhere. Kind of brings home the fact that space is out there. That it has to be *kept* out.

"You lost, kid?"

"Coming."

Facing the air lock, in the right ceiling corner along the back wall there's a small, square opening that leads to flight deck. A ladder is mounted on the wall beneath the opening—ridiculous in zero-g, but needed when on the ground. Of course, this old tub is never going Earthside again, not with all the damage to the outer hull and heat tiles that I saw on approach.

Leaving the duffel behind, I kick off for the ladder,

then yank on a rung. Too much force! I go careening through the opening, slam into the sidewall, and ricochet into the ceiling. I'm headed for a belly flop when the old spacer grabs my shirt. The wild ride ends just inches above the floor.

"Make every move slow and easy, kid, or you'll bust something." He gives my shirt a little twitch that rotates me slowly upright.

I grab a hand strap in the ceiling. The transfer of momentum twists me helplessly toward the rear of flight deck. The side and back walls should be crammed with electronic equipment, but all the consoles are gone. In the gaping black holes, the multicolored cable harnesses wave slowly in the air currents like the tentacles of sea anemones.

Through the rear windows, the capsule is visible at the end of the docking tunnel: a round lollipop on a stick, not much bigger than the golf cart. Behind it I can see the curving top of the mystery canister and the silvered spheres of the fuel and oxygen tanks poking out of the doorless cargo bay.

There's a slight jolt, and a sharp sound, like a firecracker. The shuttle lurches, then abruptly steadies when the spacer fires a stabilizer. The capsule shoots away in a puff of gas. It plunges into the atmosphere on a tight arc. Orange fire trails from it, burning away its outer shell until the internal pressure bursts it apart like a popped balloon. A thousand sparkling streamers drift toward the clouds. There go my 3-Vid goggles. I run my finger over the empty clip on my belt.

"A moment of silence for the deceased."

Now what's he talking about? I twist to face him. He's in the seat on the right, adjusting controls. The flight systems are all there and sparkling like new. That's a relief!

"Just did you a big favor, kid. It's not easy to evade TIA, but being dead helps."

"I don't understand."

"It'll be on the news tonight. Crazy old spacer out for a last joyride, didn't quite achieve orbital velocity in an ancient piece of crap. Sad. Since the cameras show you going with me, you're dead, too."

"You almost killed us for real!"

His mouth sets flat. Spoiled his fun, mentioning that. Didn't cheer me up any, either. "Strap in."

"You never *asked* me if I wanted to come."

"I gave you your chance. I told you to get lost."

"I needed your help."

"And I'm giving it to you!" He faces forward, slaps down a toggle. "We can discuss the finer moral points later. Right now, I need a clear head to get us safely out of orbit. So stop your whining and obey my orders."

I don't move from my hold on the ceiling grip. "If

you leave orbit like you dock, we haven't got a chance!"

He stops working. Without looking at me, he says in a quiet voice, "Your feelings were in control in that capsule, kid, not your head. That's bad news."

"We're talking about *you!*"

"You've got to master your feelings. Find a separate place for them. A box in your mind. Box in your heart." He traces the square frame of the keyboard on the center console between the seats. "It's the way to stay alive out here."

"So something got out of your box in the capsule?" I'm not dense. He's admitting his mistake, even as he lays these words of wisdom on me. "And now it's back in, right? I can just relax and enjoy the trip?"

He turns his head, stares with those ice-blue eyes. "You've got spunk. I like that."

He reaches for a thick book clamped to the right bulkhead. He sails it at me. I catch it and start to drift toward the rear wall from absorbing its energy. Quickly, I grab for the hand strap to anchor myself.

Spreading the book open in midair, I see that it's the preignition checklist for the main rocket motors. The thick plastic-covered pages are reassuring. If there's one thing I learned studying the first Moon missions, it's that astronauts spend a lot of time reading from checklists—long, boring lists—over and over again. They never complain. One switch in the wrong position might mean disaster. Even today, with many more automated systems, there are certain things a pilot wants to be sure of for himself.

"Another thing that keeps you alive is going by the book. That's easier with a copilot. How about it, kid?"

Copilot?

The empty chair next to him is identical to the pilot's seat. The joystick. The controls. They're connected to *real* thrusters. *Real* rockets. With the book, I can keep an eye on him. Watch for mistakes.

A little push and my feet drift over the computer terminal between the two seats. A touch on the button-studded ceiling brings my rump down into the chair. I cinch the harness buckle.

He doesn't exactly smile, but he does say kind of friendly, "Welcome aboard."

The three big monitors on the flight console display numbers and course plots. One reads TRANSLUNAR INJECTION and shows a free-return trajectory used by the Apollo Moon missions.

"You're not going to go that way, are you?"

"You recognize the course?" He sounds impressed.

"Yeah, the Apollo missions used it. The Saturn V could barely lift the Apollo stack into orbit, let alone carry enough fuel for a powered run. But there must be enough fuel in our tank to go the faster routes."

"Looks can be deceiving, kid. That tank's big, but its not full. And only one rocket motor works."

I should've guessed. "So, how long *is* it going to take us?"

"If I can get full power from that motor, I'll be able to flatten the trajectory enough to get us there in two days."

I can't believe it! I'm going to be stuck practically elbow to elbow with this guy for two days? That's long enough to have to use the toilet, and sleep, and for muscles to start going flabby. Then I see the bright side.

"But that's so slow. Won't they be able to track us?" It comes out like a question, but it's pure hope.

"Space is big, kid, really, really big. You know how hard it would be to find a ship this small?"

He's so smug, but is hc really smart enough to pull it off? He must've made a mistake, something Mark might get suspicious of, especially once the Counselor tells him about the ad. That's it!

"What about the ad? They just have to watch for a ship coming from Earth."

"We're not coming from Earth."

"What are you talking about? We're in orbit around Earth right now!"

"The guy putting up the money for this trip has a few friends at Space Command. They've fixed it so the best anyone might see is a radar shadow . . . a ghost ship . . . just right for a pair of dead men, huh?"

So someone else *is* involved in this mission. And they want to keep everything secret.

"We're not going to call Mark, are we?"

He shakes his head. "Now you're catching on."

I finally understand how it is. Nothing I want matters. I'm being shanghaied to the moon, just like thousands of men and boys in the past who got kidnapped to crew sailing ships.

He faces the controls. "Start reading at number seventy-five in the sequence."

"I could be six feet tall and read checklists. Why are you bringing me with you?"

"Like I said. Left something important on the Moon a long time ago. You're going to help me get it back."

"What is it?"

"There's no time to explain now. Read to me."

"I won't."

"Suit yourself." He keeps setting switches.

I get more and more nervous, watching. What if he's making mistakes? If I've got to go, at least I want to get out of orbit alive! "What's the next item?"

"Eighty-four," he says.

I flip the pages and scan until I find the right place. Call out, "Eighty-four. Switch D on."

"Check."

"Eighty-five. System seven on." We fall into a rhythm, like a chant. He stays half a beat ahead of me. He knows the settings by heart. I'm nothing more than backstage help, like a prompter in a play. He's different than he was in the capsule. No trouble with the buttons. No complaints from the computer. But he's not faced with a crisis. There's no pressure. No need for quick decisions or lightning reflexes.

"One hundred twenty: fuel tank A valve to on."

"Check."

Monotonous stuff. Our voices drone on, bringing an echo of other voices with that special quality only heard between astronauts and mission control. Steady voices full of letters and numbers recited in the cool monotone of professionals.

I feel as if I've done this before.

"One hundred seventy, intermix heater switch D to on."

"Check."

But of course, in a way, I have. In simulators. In the hundreds of 3-Vids I've watched. There are always scenes just like this. Even in my dreams.

"Two hundred: igniter switches to on." And yet, the echo shadowing our voices seems different, almost like the start of a squiggly.

"Check."

"Two hundred four: lock ignition circuit into NavComp."

He runs a systems check of the NavComp. That's the master computer in charge of integrating every aspect of the flight plan. The NavComp's most important job is to coordinate the maneuvering thrusters to keep the ship on course no matter what else is happening.

"Check."

My fingers slip turning the last plastic page. That unwelcome feeling of nausea starts in my stomach. Scared. Plain and simple. I want to go to the Moon, but not with this old spacer in this old tub. As long as we're in orbit, I have some options. He could drop me off at Olympus Space Station. I might be able to get a message to Dad and Mark before they hear the news.

"Lose your tongue?" There's challenge in his voice. He knows I'm scared. Why shouldn't I be? He hasn't even told me his name, let alone what this mission is all about!

"I'm sorry. I don't want to go."

"You want to be a pilot, don't you? This is the way. What other kid can get his hands on the controls of a real shuttle, huh?"

"I haven't touched the controls!"

"Long journey ahead. It'll happen." He completes the checklist without my help. "Lean back."

The big green digits on the countdown clock light up.

10-9-8-

The instruments come alive as the FlightComp makes the final check—last chance to scrub if anything is wrong.

5-4-

Strong vibrations as the turbo pumps kick on. I clench my right hand into a fist. Clamp my jaw in expectation . . .

2-1-

IGNITION

The power of the rocket motor slams through the ancient frame. Metal creaks and strains as the thrust builds. A support strut moans right next to my ear. The invisible hand of acceleration squeezes my chest again. I sink deeper into the padded seat. My hand isn't hurting. I'm going to be okay this time.

I glance sideways. His eyes are closed and his cheeks are all scrunched up. Looks like he's in pain, then I realize he's *grinning* with the same moronic joy I felt flying through middeck.

I want that! Close my eyes. Pretend. A real spaceship! Heading for the stars! The cockpit of a sporty Comet Catcher . . .

Impossible. New rattles and bangs shiver the hull and grow louder every second. Sounds like I have my ear against a pipe and a hundred maniacs are hammering on it. The ship is going to fall apart! Need that space suit. Need it to stop!

IGNITION PLUS 40.

Halfway through the burn. The thrust piles on, like shovelfuls of sand. The green numbers fade. A darkness spreads behind my eyes. A sense of danger. Of something nightmarish. I don't want to go there. I mustn't.

I feel another scream starting to build. It's got nothing to do with pain this time. It's pure scared trying to get out. I can't disgrace myself again. I jam a fist to my mouth, bite down on a finger.

Just when I think I can't hold the scream back any longer, the acceleration ceases. The blackness flies away, taking the fear with it. The center monitor tells us:

IGNITION PLUS 81

VELOCITY CONSTANT

TRANSLUNAR INJECTION COMPLETED

Nick of time. Never thought I'd be such a wimp.

8

MISSION TIME

T plus 02:01:08

THE soft click of keys draws my attention. The old spacer asks for a status report. In front of me, #3 monitor shows all systems green. Kind of amazing, considering the sounds this tub made.

He says, "*Old Glory*'s no Valadium Thruster, but she'll get us there."

This derelict doesn't even come close to the power of the Lance Ramjet. I'm ashamed to think how I boasted to him about wanting to feel those engines. I barely got through this burn. A stinking *space shuttle* . . .

Maybe it's just the situation, this whole day. Got me rattled. Wasn't he worried about shock?

"*Old Glory*? Didn't they call the flag that once?"

"Who says I named her for the flag? Maybe it's for

when she rode fire from Earth. Maybe it's for me. Lot of old glory around here, kid."

"Lot of *old,* that's for sure."

Bing bing bing.

The alarm sounds gentle, so you aren't scared to death, but both of us freeze for a heartbeat.

Then he's all head motions, searching the consoles for a red light. Me, too, but most of the lights don't mean anything to me.

Bing bing bing.

"There!" He jabs the flashing red button and a 3-D graphic of the shuttle—complete with wing holes—flickers onto #1 monitor in front of him. The graph shows the hull surfaces, shaded to indicate temperature differences. Frosty purple underside. Yellows, reds, and white—superhot!—topside.

Something's really wrong! The hull should be a uniform temperature; orange all over.

Bing bing bing.

He toggles on #2 monitor in the center of the console. It displays the temperature map for the cargo bay. The tanks are white as blank paper, superheated. I yell, "They're gonna blow!"

He grabs the joystick, jerks it hard, kicking the shuttle over. With an easy flick and twist of his wrist, he counteracts the roll so the underside stays pointed sunward. Never saw that kind of skill in the capsule.

Bing bing bing.

A crackling noise, like dry pine twigs burning, filters inside from the hull. The yellows and reds cool quickly into orange, shading to grays. The purple warms toward orange. The tanks are still white-hot; still in the danger zone.

Bing bing bing.

Neither of us breathes. The silvery insulation is our enemy now, trapping the heat inside the tanks. If the heat doesn't bleed off quickly enough, if the fuel gasifies, we'll be blown to atoms.

A blush of red appears on the tanks as the temperature continues to cool, spreads slowly over the spheres. Time seems to pass slowly, like watching a tomato ripen, but really only a few seconds pass before the alarm stops.

"You forgot to spin us!" In space, you have to spin a ship for even heating, like a chicken in a rotisserie. The first astronauts called it the barbecue roll. Basic stuff.

"Not me—this!" His arm jabs upward, smacks the corner of the NavComp in the ceiling between us. The most important computer on the ship and it screwed up! "It should have rolled us automatically."

We were nearly killed by a computer glitch!

The brushed aluminum faceplate shows only green lights, glowing and pulsing in a normal rhythm as if to say, "Me? Nothing wrong with me." But something *is* wrong with it, to have skipped such an important maneuver in the flight plan.

He runs a diagnostic. The NavComp says everything's fine. We can't trust the diagnostic. I remind him, "It passed during the preflight check, too."

"I remember." He sounds a lot less upset than he should be. "*Old Glory*'s a planet hugger, kid. Some spacers get sloppy when help is just over the horizon at a space station."

"We're nowhere near a space station now! Turn back!"

He looks at me like I just cut a fart. "Tell me you know better than that."

U-turns in space aren't easy to do. You need special ships and a lot of spare fuel. When the oxygen tank blew on *Apollo 13,* they had to ride it out all the way to the Moon. That's our level of technology in this old rust bucket.

"Then what *do* we do?"

"Run some better diagnostics. Watch the NavComp like a hawk to make sure it doesn't skip any more commands in the flight plan." He turns back to the controls.

"Well, look at that." He points to #1 monitor. It displays our projected course and an estimated time of arrival of 44:21:08. Even during the crisis, the NavComp was busy calculating the results of the translunar injection burn. "It can't be too screwed up. Shaved nearly four hours off our ETA."

"If we can believe it," I mutter.

He purses his lips. "That's a point. I'll verify soon as I spin this baby."

The tanks show orange now. He works the joystick and the display shuttle slowly tilts perpendicular to our line of flight. The same thing is happening to the real one, but there's no sense of motion inside. Sunlight flares into flight deck, hot and bright. A thruster belches. The shuttle begins to spin on its long axis from nose to rocket cones. The sunlight winks out. Earth passes across our view, the swift flicker of a bluebird through the marsh grasses. Sunlight gushes, blinding.

"Pull your shades." He draws the ones on his side, then hits a button that closes the rear window shutters. I close my shades. The rapid strobe of light and dark would drive you crazy. "I'm behind schedule, so sit quiet and let me work."

"What did you bring me for, if you just want me to sit here?"

"Keep interrupting me and you'll never find out." He unfolds a star chart and spreads it in the air between us like a curtain. When he takes his hands away, it hangs there as if tacked to the air. Keys click, but I can't see what he's doing.

Sitting quiet isn't easy. There's this electricity in me. I want to tear that chart to pieces. Make him take me home.

Forcing myself to stay still makes me aware of a good reason to get moving. I unsnap the harness.

He peels aside an edge of the chart. "Where you going?"

"To pee." A small flick of my toe on the deck and an elbow jab against the cushions set me drifting into the small, open space behind the seats.

"Hey!" He grabs my ankle.

I kick, crinkling the chart, but can't get free. Chin tucked against my chest, I look back along the length of my floating body at him. "What?"

"On my ship, you ask permission to leave your post."

"Like in school? Raise my hand to go to the bathroom?"

"No game, kid." The circle of his fingers tightens around my ankle. "There's only one captain. One man giving orders. Understand?"

The words come from a place of stone inside him. I nod.

"Good." He lets go. "Know how to use the toilet?"

Nod. I tuck my legs, float up near the ceiling.

"You know a lot for a kid who claims he's never been to space before."

"Because I'm studying—"

"Drop the act, will you?"

"Act? What act?"

"I know who you are . . . Stewart Edward Hale."

9

MISSION TIME

T plus 03:22:09

MY scalp goes prickly. The Counselor thought it was really important that I never told this guy my name. Is he a stalker? Was he planning to kidnap me all along? My voice almost catches as I ask, "How do you know who I am?"

"Talked to the janitor at the TransHub. So tell me," he goes on, frowning, "why did you lie about having been in space before? People value experience. Remember that, next job interview."

Why is this guy always coming at me from a strange and distant planet? "I *didn't* lie! I've tried *everything* to make Dad take me off planet. And if he had taken me, I would never have given *you* a second thought."

"I could have sworn—" A flash of puzzlement, then his face ices over. "My mistake. Dismissed."

A little push on the ceiling sends me feetfirst

through the hatch into middeck. I'm just as eager to disappear as he is to see me go. That was a pretty rotten thing to say to him, but hey, so what? He deserves to be confronted with the hard truth. He keeps doing it to me.

I'm not thrilled about confronting the toilet, though. I drift slowly toward it. Space toilets can be tricky. At least I'm a boy. It's even trickier for girls.

There are handles and footholds so you can keep your bum well anchored to the seat. Air suction replaces the pull of gravity. To pee you use a special tube that looks just like a vacuum cleaner hose. I wiggle my feet into the straps, then flip the switch. The motor even sounds like a vacuum cleaner. That's a little nerve-wracking. I test the suction against my palm.

"Hey kid!" His yell almost startles the tube out of my hand. "Bring some Gunk and Squirt when you come back. You'll find it in the bag."

I finish up and switch off the horrible noise.

The duffel rests in a back corner, pinned near the deck by a twisted locker door. As I glide over to it, my feet rotate toward the ceiling. I catch the zipper, drag it open with my momentum, bump to a stop against the lockers. Hovering, I check out the contents. A huge number of squeeze bottles, labeled whiskey, are clustered in the folds of a heavy blanket.

Enough alcohol here to fuel a small rocket!

Under the blanket are packets, some full of squishy green stuff that looks like pureed spinach, others translucent and watery. Gunk and Squirt. Emergency rations. I tasted samples at the museum. Yuck!

Pushing aside the packets, my fingers brush canvas. Nothing else? He can't carry *everything* in that jacket. I rummage toward one end, then the other, find something square-edged hidden by the blanket: a stack of thin folders. They're trussed together with a bit of old fuel hose that still smells of hydrazine. The covers are real leather, though, fine and smooth. Ten in all, identical. Sandwiched in the middle is something else, much thicker. Looks like a book.

I cock an ear toward flight deck. Clicks. A beep. He's busy.

A tweak on the hose sets the stack floating free. It spins slowly in front of my face. A cube, about the size of the bread maker I used for the jack-in-the-box. Something glitters on the bottom. I clutch the stack, rotate it. In gold letters, the words: Pilot Achievement Award. Beneath the words, the insignia of Alldrives Space Systems Corporation is embossed into the leather.

Awards? For *piloting*? From Alldrives?

I can't believe it. It must've been long ago. He sure is a screwup now! He didn't rip those insignias off. I bet he was drummed out of the service. For drinking on duty. For incompetence.

A trip to the Moon shouldn't be this dangerous. Someone's got to rescue me.

But no one's even looking. They think I'm dead.

Tears start. I don't try to stop them. Everything goes blurry as the tears puddle deeper and deeper over my eyeballs. They don't run like on Earth. I blink. Two tiny wet blobs pop into the air in front of my nose. Nearly cross-eyed, I watch them undulate as if something inside is struggling to escape. Slowly, the tears quiet into perfect spheres.

My eyes stare, helplessly wide wide open, unseeing. I circle my arm over them, creating a comfortable darkness. My face feels puffy. Bloat. My body's adjusting to zero-g.

Head hurts. Not my cheek, though. His soda icing idea worked.

I can't go back to flight deck. Can't deal with his craziness anymore. Easier just to stretch out and make a bed on the thin, stale air. No pressure anywhere on my body—no mattress under me or covers over. The lack of normal sensation brings home a fact I lost track of in all this craziness: I'm in zero-g!

And on my way to the Moon!

And he said I'd get to fly this thing. Piece of junk, but it does have a real rocket motor. Real thrusters.

My dream come true . . .

Too bad it's turned out to be a nightmare.

10

MISSION TIME

T plus 09:45:10

WHAT *do you think? Mom asks.*

A Tyrannosaurus looms above me. "Too many teeth."

Mom takes my hand. "Well, you braved the terrors of the Paleozoic. Reward time."

"Rockets!"

We turn a corner into a dead-end corridor. There's a red door at the end. Something's wrong. This isn't the way to the rocket room.

"Stop, Mom." Mom starts running toward the door. It opens. Smoke pours out. "No, Mom, no!"

I try to run after her, but I can't move. My legs and arms thrash, rub against something slick and confining.

"Hey! Kid! Hey! Wake up!"

The old spacer's voice is a splash of cold water. My

eyes pop open—floor under my head; feet lost in the light.

"Easy! It's just a sock!"

Sock. Sleep restraint.

I stop struggling and pull my chin in against my throat. I'm Velcroed to the wall, my body hidden in the white cocoon of the sock. He's in the corner, head and shoulders poking through the ceiling hatch. Both of us are upside down, but that would only matter on Earth. I come fully awake into the cheerless zero-g reality of middeck.

"How'd I get in this?"

"Couldn't wake you. Couldn't leave you drifting around, either."

So he tucked me in. Nice of him. Then it dawns on me—I was completely vulnerable! Yanking an arm out, I pull at the Velcro seam. The sock peels open. I'm still in all my clothes, even my sneakers. Tucking my legs toward my chest, I roll out of the sock. My brain swims.

"Ugh."

Grabbing at a hand strap, I park myself on the floor. The room spins. My head is stuffy, like I've been standing on it for hours. But that's only an illusion. No real up and down in zero-g. My mouth tastes of cotton. Teeth feel sleep-slimed. No toothbrush.

"How long have I been asleep?"

"About six hours."

"Six hours! What time is it?"

"Planetside, about eighteen hundred hours, EST."

Six o'clock in the evening. It's hard to believe only nine hours have passed since I ran away from Mrs. Phillips. It's still my birthday. The party was supposed to start around now. They must know what happened with the Counselor; they've probably even heard the news about the PLV by now. Mark. Dad. Everyone.

The old spacer's head and shoulders dip through the hatch. A hand reaches into middeck, shoots something my way. "Take those with as much water as you can drink."

I catch the small packet. It contains three aspirin-sized yellow pills. "What are they?"

"For the space sickness. Get rid of bloat. Chase away hallucinations."

"Oh." Guess I was screaming out loud again.

"Don't worry about it, kid. Happens to some people." He looks at a clipboard, flips a couple pages. Paper! He's actually using printouts.

"Don't you even have a FlexyPad to write on?"

"Too vulnerable to snooping."

He's careful. Like an OmniLink, FlexyPads are network active and locatable. We're very *alone* out here.

"Take a half hour for breakfast. Then one hour of exercise."

I have to exercise to keep up my muscle tone. They say a day in zero-g is like spending two days flat on your back in bed. Muscles start going slack right away. Even after a few days in orbit, the early astronauts could barely walk when they returned.

He flips a page. "Then one hour of training. After that, you go on watch and I sleep."

"Training? For what?"

"Let's keep that a surprise—for your birthday."

He starts to drift away. "Wait a minute. I never told you today's my birthday."

"Know your name, kid. You can find out a lot about a person once you know that."

"What's your name?"

"Fred," he says and disappears into flight deck.

Fred. Right. I don't believe him for a minute. Where's the duffel? Casting a glance around middeck, I see it neatly lashed to the locker wall. Might be some answers in there. I'll take another look when he's asleep.

Right now I need that water. Can't let dehydration get a grip on me. The way this guy likes to throw me off balance, I'll need a clear head to outsmart him.

The water dispenser is on the wall opposite the toilet. I lean in its direction and push off, brake to a stop in front of it with a light touch of fingers against the wall. A dozen sip tubes bristle the faceplate. One is labeled "Stewart." The other actually says "Fred."

I tug the length of tubing out, flip the seal open, and take a tiny sip, expecting stale and brackish water. But it's cold and clean tasting. I gulp down a gallon, at least! A person dehydrates fast in space. That's why he wanted me to drink a lot with the pills.

I finger the hard pills. Wish I could be sure they'd only keep away the scary parts—like that red door. I would love not to see that again, but the early part with the dinosaur . . . that seemed more like a memory than a squiggle.

Unsure whether to take the pills or not, I slip them into my pants pocket. Ouch! The folded paper corner of the Space Academy Camp application jabs a cuticle. No way I'll make it to the Moon before Dad leaves. He'll start back to Earth as soon as he hears the news, won't he? We'll pass like ships in the night. Unless I could get him a message somehow.

The intercom sputters. "Forgot to mention, kid. Try the cocoa. It's good. Twenty minutes until exercise time."

I check out the galley next to the water dispenser. The only item *in* the drinks section is cocoa. A food rack holds packets of Gunk and Squirt.

He's been busy. Clipboards. Schedules. A regular

Mr. Efficiency. Pulled his act together? Doesn't matter. He's only half the danger. How many mistakes did the NavComp make while I was asleep? What might go *pop* next?

I reach for the cocoa button. The intercom speaker catches my eye—*radio!* Everything's happened so fast, it never crossed my mind to look for a radio. But there's got to be one. When he's asleep, I'll find it, get a message off. With any luck, maybe Dad's ship could intercept us. Even if it can't, at least they'll know I'm not dead.

They must have the news by now. Were they swarmed by reporters, like after Mom crashed?

FATHER DRIVES SON TO SUICIDAL LENGTHS TO FULFILL SPACEFLIGHT DREAM.

Suddenly, the mesh of the intercom speaker expands, the holes grow dark and menacing. Oh no! A squiggly. Not here . . . not with him . . . not in space! But there's nothing to stop it and I fall into . . .

A microphone practically up my nose. I can see every dark dimple in the wire mesh. The reporter is asking how it feels to know your mom saved all those people.

My dead mom.

Lips squeeze tight, refusing to answer him. I grow small, smaller. Fall into one of the tiny dimples in the microphone . . .

. . . and come back on middeck.

Whoa! Catch myself up short, about to pitch over toward the deck. My lips are pressed tight together, locked in that refusal to talk to the reporter.

The scar throbs in time to my accelerated pulse.

Remembering!

I've *never* remembered such a vivid detail about the crash before! It's what I've always wanted, but it was horrible . . .

I press my hand over the pills in my pocket. The plastic crinkles. If I'm going to start falling into microphone dimples, I may have to take them. But what if it's something good next time, something with Mom like the tree house, or the science museum?

Guess I'll wait and see.

11

MISSION TIME
T plus 11:01:11

MIDDECK smells like a sewer. I used the toilet right after breakfast, *before* exercising. That was a mistake. The suction is supposed to keep the toilet from stinking. I don't know why I thought it would work right on this tub.

I'm pacing the workout to keep my breathing shallow and to favor my hand. The scar is really tender today. Usually I don't mind exercising, but between the stink and this primitive machine, sticking to the program hasn't been easy. There isn't even a 3-Vid hookup!

The intercom sputters. "Fifteen more minutes, kid. Pick up that pace, you're slacking off again."

That's the third time he's gotten on my case. I thrust my legs once more, then freeze. The tension-springs twang from that final burst of angry power. Exercise is important, but I'm not going to jump every time this guy says so.

I pop the seat belt and twist myself out of the stupid machine. It's like a spider's web with all the bars and cables and springs. After forty-five minutes in its clutches, I feel like a stuck bug. I toe the control switch. The machine collapses into its storage compartment under the floor, restoring a little room to move around in middeck.

The clatter sounds my defiance. What will he do?

There's a rip of Velcro from flight deck. He flows through the floor hatch, his body gently rotating like a lazy mobile. A toe flick against the wall gives him a perfect glide path for the air lock. He hauls the hatch open without even a wince. He hasn't cursed once since we've been in zero-g. Must feel like a bird who's had a broken wing returning to the sky.

"Come on." He ducks into the tunnel. A moment later, another hatch clatters. Looks like I'm going to find out what's in that canister in the cargo bay.

I thrust off, correct my course with a little touch on the air lock hatch, and glide through the middle chamber into the opposite tunnel. But he's still half in the tunnel. I make a hasty grab at a handhold and jerk to a stop face-to-face with the soles of his shoes.

He's changed his street shoes for Velcro booties. I need to do that, then I could get a solid grip on the carpeted walls as easily as he does.

I hear the buzz and snap of lights coming on, then he floats into the canister, unblocking the tunnel. Sweet air flows over me. Through the round portal I see a hammock of fine mesh shock webbing slung the length of the canister. The webbing bulges in the middle, hiding something the size of a refrigerator.

The canister itself is a long, narrow cylinder about the size of a classroom. Two light strips line the sides. Attached to the curving wall near the middle is a control console and, next to it, an anchor boom.

I slip in and breathe deep. Sweet! I reach to close the hatch, but he grabs the handle, stopping me.

"Never seal all personnel on the wrong side of an air lock, kid. Something happens, jams the hatch, you're trapped away from the controls."

"I didn't know."

"Now you do."

He glides to the control console opposite the bulge in the shock webbing, then swivels the anchor boom out. Parting the web, he attaches the boom to whatever's inside. Coming back to the forward wall, he unhooks the end of the webbing, then launches himself to the far side. As he flies past the thing, he strips off the webbing with a bullfighter's flourish to unveil a tiny ship. It looks like a turkey baster with tentacles.

"A squid! I can't believe it. Where do you *find* this stuff?"

"Flea markets."

"Yeah, right, and this was owned by a little old lady who only flew it to Mars once a year."

"She's all yours now, kid. Happy birthday!"

"You didn't get that for me! You didn't even *know* me until yesterday."

"True. But I had someone *like* you in mind. Loosen up. Check her out. Santa never left you anything like this little beauty."

"It's just a robot. What am I supposed to do with it?"

"Not anymore. Take a closer look."

I'm almost afraid to, but I push off, angling out over the squid. The ascent stage is an elongated teardrop shape. The descent stage bulges around a big rocket nozzle and has long, thin landing struts sweeping backward like tentacles, giving these ships their nicknames—squids. Officially, they were known as AMDs—automated mining drones—and were used for sampling asteroids in the belt.

This one's been modified. There's a window near the nose. The robotic drilling arm is gone, replaced by two tubes like you might use to send a big poster through the mail. A large oval opening has been cut into the side. I catch the rim of it with my foot, flip, and poke my head inside. It looks like a miniature cockpit. He's turned this into a lunar lander! It's rigged to fly, with just enough empty space for a midget or one short kid . . .

I pull my head out quick. "You want *me* to land this on the Moon?"

"You're the backup. I'll fly her down on remote."

"And hit the Moon as hard as we hit the dock? No way!"

"Still think you're better than me?" He's floating near the simulation control console, arms and legs crossed like a Buddha. His ponytail sticks straight out from his head, like a stub of whisk broom. "Get in."

He yanks a flat screen monitor from the console and drifts toward the squid trailing control cables like the tail of a kite.

I hesitate. He's pissed. Reminding him about that terrible docking wasn't so smart. He'll throw me a simulation full of problems. I won't have a chance.

But this *is* a spaceship. Once I learn to fly it, I could go anywhere, not just where he wants . . .

I slip inside. My arms are pinned at my sides with only a few inches of free space between my body and the hull. My hands come to rest on two control boxes.

Exploring the boxes by feel, my fingers find a joystick on the right one. That's a handicap, since the scar is feeling so tender today. The other box is covered with the standard three by four numeric keypad. Miniature instruments rim the window and show things like pitch, altitude, fuel, drop speed, and forward speed. About as bare-bones as the PLV capsule, this thing doesn't even have a heads-up display!

"Okay, kid." His voice squeaks through a speaker near my ear. "Simple sequence: boost clear, deorbit burn and free-fall to eight miles, powered descent to five thousand feet, pitchover and go for landing."

The sequence seems familiar, but before I can figure out why, he's explaining the control codes. The numeric codes turn out to be the standard ones used by most of the simulators I've played around in. Maybe I have a chance after all.

With my eyes closed, I review the code sequences, walking my fingertips over the keypad. A sudden rip, clank, and clatter startles me. He's duct taping the flat screen to the outside of the window. The screen flickers on. It maps the surface of the Moon as if from a great height. The screen is crooked and the simulation is lousy. The shadows are muddy. The surface features, which should have sharp, clear edges, are blurred. Compared to the HOOPscope image, this is like a drawing done with blunt crayons.

"Boost away," he calls as the simulation starts running.

I fire a lateral jet to thrust the squid clear. A splutter of static comes out of the speaker. Guess that's the sound effects. There's no sense of motion or thrust. Piece of junk. I have to read the instruments and *imagine* what's happening. Makes it hard to feel really involved.

If this were for real, the squid would be orbiting with the long axis parallel to the surface and the rocket nozzle facing forward. That's why the screen scrolls the changing moonscape from the bottom. The nose window would be turned toward the surface and I'd be lying on my belly looking down at it. At pitchover, all that changes. Pitchover is a tricky maneuver that rotates the ship from parallel flight into a perpendicular attitude to aim the nozzle straight at the surface. That allows the final hover and braking for landing.

"Begin DOI," he says, then adds, "That's descent orbit initiation, kid."

"I know what it is." My first test . . . and a chance to impress this guy. Quickly scanning the relevant numbers on the instruments, I calculate the proper burn duration for the descent arc. I lock in my answers and fire the engine. If I've got it wrong, I'll plunge out of orbit.

A wimpy raspberry warbles from the speaker. The meters show forward speed dropping sharply. The slower orbital speed lets the Moon's gravity get a stronger grip on the squid. The altimeter registers a rapid descent from my initial orbit fifty miles up. Eight miles above the surface, the readings stabilize at perilune, the lowest point in my new orbit. Perfect work.

"Okay, kid, power down to five thousand feet."

I reignite the engine and throttle up until the drop rate increases to nearly a mile a minute. About three miles up, the display clicks in at the same scale as the ceiling map in my bedroom. Suddenly, the mysterious landscape of craters and shadows transforms. That's the Sea of Tranquility down there! A square edge comes into view. I squint to sharpen the details. The perimeter fence! Tranquility Base! *That's* why the landing sequence sounded familiar. I'm retracing the flight path taken by the *Eagle* on the first Moon landing!

Did he pick this simulation at random, or is that where he's sending me?

"Five thousand!"

I'm supposed to do something.

"Pitchover!"

Oh, right. I have to rotate the squid and brake for landing.

"Do it!" A small firecracker goes off next to my ear. The squid jiggles. He's pounding on the hull! He does it again.

I flinch and jab a thruster by accident. The nose flips. Stars craters stars craters blink on the monitor as the squid cartwheels out of control. Red lights dance around the window.

"What the . . . stabilize!"

I try, but the rapid black-white flicker of the monitor makes me dizzy.

"Cut main thrust!" His urgent voice drills into me.

I do. The cartwheeling stops, but not the spin. I fire a thruster to counteract it. Wrong one. The squid rotates faster. The display strobes into a frenzy of shattered light.

"The other one!" He whaps the hull. "The other one!"

He's so worked up; this is *real* for him. I lay on the right thruster until the spin stops.

"Nozzle forward! Hurry!"

My mistakes have flung me at the surface! The squid is down to a thousand feet before I get the nozzle aimed right.

"Full throttle!"

Ram it to one hundred percent. A warning buzzer: low fuel.

I've been here before—out of luck. My hands automatically drop and drift away from the controls in defeat.

"Lateral! More lateral!"

He's still trying to save this landing. Before I can figure out what he means, I'm the newest crater on the Moon.

A fierce grip closes on my ankle. He yanks me out. It feels like being sucked down a drain. My chin thumps the instrument board, ribs rake over the opening. He lets go. Helpless, I tumble, then crash against the wall. Flailing on the rebound, I snatch a landing strut and hold tight.

"Why didn't you lateral? You could've made it!" He glares across the engine nozzle. The veins in his neck bulge hugely. His forehead glistens with sweat. Crazy as Mark's basketball coach. Even during practice, he acts like the world has ended if you miss a foul shot.

I rub my ribs. "That *hurt!*"

"Not as much as hitting the Moon will hurt!"

"It's your fault I messed up."

"How do you figure that?"

"I lost my concentration when I recognized Tranquility Base. That wouldn't have happened if you just *told* me! Everything's a secret with you."

"You're a sharp one, kid, I'll hand you that."

"So that *is* where you're sending me. Why?"

"Why won't matter if you can't land."

"I'll do better next time."

"There isn't a next time!" He lunges for me. I dodge, but he pivots over the landing struts and catches my wrist. He slaps my hand against the cold metal skin.

"Feel her, kid." I try to pull my hand away. He holds it there, a commanding look in his eye. "She'll take you to the Moon and back *if* you become a part of her. Otherwise, she'll kill you."

As if I wasn't already in enough danger! My gaze follows down his forearm, where gray hairs stand upright from tensed muscles. The ship's thin skin dimples under my hand. A crash landing would shred it. The shrapnel would rip open the space suit of anyone inside.

Decompression. Lungs ripped inside out. Blood boiling.

My gaze slides, fixes on a thruster. I close my eyes, feel my way back into what was happening, spin out a series of maneuvering options . . .

"I guess I should've skimmed with a little lateral thrust."

"That's the idea." He lets go. "Get in. Try again."

I flex my right hand. Little zaps from stressed

nerves shoot across the scarred palm. "I'd do better with the joystick on the left. Can you change it?"

"Maybe. Why?"

"This bothers me sometimes." I show him my right hand.

He winces, then looks at his Chronomatrix. "Not enough time now. Next session. What happened anyway?"

"When I was little . . ." I stop myself from repeating Dad's story. Because if I don't remember it, how can I be sure it's true?

"Actually, I don't know."

12

MISSION TIME

T plus 12:08:12

WE'RE out of time. Come on."

He powers down the simulator. We've done three more landing attempts . . . resulting in two crashes and an explosion that blew up the squid *and* the shuttle when I fired the ascent engine instead of a thruster. Too bad the simulator is such a dud; that would've been something to experience in virtual reality!

I twist out of the squid and stretch. Sure feels good to *move!* Despite the failures, I'm feeling upbeat about how things went. It's my typical learning curve with a new ship, but he's not happy. He's floating near the hatch of the canister wearing a sour expression. The only thing he said to me after each simulation was "try again."

Would've been great if things had clicked right

away—surprise *him* for a change. But so what? I don't need to impress him. I got the basics down. I could fly away in the squid if my plan to find the radio and call for help doesn't work out.

I launch myself toward that end of the canister, doing somersaults as I go. Reaching the wall, I make like a swimmer about to turn a lap, but instead of pushing off, I let my knees absorb the momentum. I stick there like Spider-Man, four feet from the hatch. He stares at me, a look of surprise mingled with . . . relief?

"What's the matter?"

"Nothing. Just didn't know if you had that kind of spacial sense in you or not. I'm glad to see you do." He shuts off the lights in the canister and ducks into the tunnel.

I follow him, closing the hatch behind me.

He soars across mid-deck and stops at a control panel near the ladder. He shuts off the lights in mid-deck, then glides through the hatch into the glow from flight deck. I'm right behind him.

Even on flight deck, he's got half the lights shut off. When I settle into my seat, I notice a few consoles are dark, too. One of them is the radio. It's on his side of the cockpit. I'd practically have to crawl into his lap to get to it.

"What's with the lights?"

"Fuel cell failed. Have to conserve power." He pulls a clipboard off its Velcro wall hanger.

The fuel cells make electricity by combining hydrogen and oxygen gas. The "waste" is pure water. That's what we drink from the dispenser and why it tastes so clean even in this tub.

"How many are left?"

"Four."

No big deal then. He's just being cautious, since a couple are usually spares. We go back to worrying about our real problem. Like two anxious parents after a feeding, we wait for the NavComp to execute the next maneuver—come on, baby, burp.

Beep. The prompt alerts us to pay attention.

"There she goes." He checks the sequence off on his printout.

"Burp."

"Huh?"

"Nothing."

"Get serious, kid. It's your watch." He hands me the clipboard, draws his finger down the columns of the mission profile. "Time here. Maneuver sequence here. Verify on monitor two. Check off here."

I'm glad he thinks I'm goofing off. Mission time is 12:18:16. The first maneuver I have to verify will happen in fifteen minutes. The next one is an hour after that. That gap ought to give me enough time to use the radio. Unless he isn't asleep by then.

"You going to sleep now?"

"Cocktail hour first." He reaches for the jacket stuffed between the armrest and the bulkhead. Passed out would be even better than asleep. But the bottle is only half-full. I doubt that's enough to do it. He takes a sip, then looks at the clock. Again and again, like one of those water-filled bobbing ducks.

"Wouldn't you be more comfortable in a sock?"

"I'm fine right here, thanks."

He's going to stay up, make sure I get the first check right. What am I going to do for the next fifteen minutes—watch him drink? I tap the Navcomp with the edge of the clipboard. "Any games in this thing?"

"Solitaire."

"That's more boring than being bored!"

"You shouldn't be playing games anyway. You should be training."

"Hey, I'm willing. It's not *my* fault I have to babysit this piece of junk."

"True enough. I don't have any training routines on the system here. I'll transfer some from the squid later. You're not as good as I expected."

I shrug. "I always crash a lot."

"Because you fly it like a computer."

"That's all I've ever flown! Dad won't—"

"You told me." His eyes go back to the clock.

"Why do you keep doing that? It'll beep when it's time."

"I'm not waiting for the maneuver." He takes a big pull on the straw. "It's a special day for me, too."

"It's your birthday?!"

He shakes his head. "An anniversary coming up in a minute."

"You're married?"

"Not that kind."

"What kind, then?"

"Sorry, kid, that's one of those things I've gotta keep locked in a box." He drains the bottle with a bubbly slurp, crushing it to get the last drop. He digs out another one and quickly sucks half of it down.

"This isn't exactly a great day for me, either." Going to the Moon ought to be the best birthday present ever.

"Keep your mind on your job, kid. It'll help."

Beep.

I verify the maneuver and check it off. Next one in an hour.

"She's all yours now." He slips the bottle into a holder, then reaches for a pair of blackout eyeshades clipped to the ceiling. "Wake me in four hours."

"Is that enough?" I don't want him sleep deprived.

"Don't need much sleep these days. A perk of old age."

"How old *are* you?"

"Hundred twenty-one Earth years. Seventy-six the way spacers figure it."

"That's a big difference." He's either traveled super fast, so that relativity effects slowed time, or been out on long, slow trips in cryogenic suspension. Maybe both.

"Been a spacer a long time, kid. Long, long time." He pauses a moment, thinking something over. "After that trip to Venus, you couldn't drag me back to Earth with a black hole."

"Hey, Val Thorsten said that in Venus: Inferno Below the Clouds."

"I know. They stuck to the truth in the early ones."

"What do you mean? The 3-Vids are docudramas. They're all true."

"Ah, the innocence of babes . . ." He shakes his head. "You might find some bits of real history in them, if you look hard enough. But I never chased pirates. Never with Tony. Never with Bob. Never after the Jupiter disaster."

Oh great! Now he thinks he's Val Thorsten!

He brings the bottle to his lips.

A deadbeat like him, borrowing Val's glory. I'm insulted on Val's behalf. Should I challenge him, or just play along? The more he talks, the more he drinks.

I want him drunk. "So what happened on the way to Jupiter?"

He broods over the straw. His mouth draws into a thin, hard line. Another long pull. "Damned Photrino drive. Trouble from the first. Old Man Lance saved a few nickels and Tony . . . Tony paid full price."

His voice softens, apologetic. Tony is Val's chief engineer, and his cheerful face comes clearly to mind from Asteroid Run. I don't remember Old Man Lance in Jupiter Turnabout, but the new Photrino drive *was* skittish. It conked out during the most critical maneuver. That left Val, his crew, and the two hundred colonists with no hope of ever reaching Jupiter.

"No hope of Jupiter. Just one chance to get home. Tony had to fix . . ."

I can see every detail of the scene where Val talks with Tony about trying a very tricky, very dangerous boomerang maneuver. The drive had to work perfectly. But the fusion bottle collapsed. Tony had to go into the fusion chamber even though the damper fields were unstable.

This guy says the 3-Vid is a fake, but he's describing it exactly like it happened. A chill goes down my spine. Could he really be . . .

No. He's a fan, like me. He's just retelling the 3-Vid and casting himself as Val Thorsten. I do it all the time myself.

He comes to the part where there are just two repairs left. The damper fields start to fail. Val stands ready to pull Tony out—

". . . but nobody could get him out . . ."

"No! That's not true!"

"Damn it, kid, who're you going to believe?" His hand slams my chest and twists up a fistful of shirt. He pulls me half out of my seat and over the center console that separates us. Our noses almost touch. His angry eyes are the pale blue of pond ice. His breath smells explosive. "Tony *died* in there!"

"That's crazy, I just saw him in Asteroid Run."

"Lies!" He shoves me away. My shoulder slams the bulkhead. I stiff-arm the center console to stop the rebound, then settle sideways in the seat, back hunched against the hull, knees drawn up against my chest for protection.

Maybe it was a mistake, wanting him drunk. No. It's working. He's sucking on the bottle again.

I just have to be more careful how I react. The idea of Tony dead caught me by surprise, that's all. I just blurted out what I thought. But he gets violent as well as crazy. My karate won't be much good here. So many of the moves depend on gravity.

Some of the whiskey beads at the corner of his mouth and spills into the air. He swipes at his wet lips, clumsy.

He really is a sad old bum.

Slowly, his finger comes toward my forehead. I pull back. The finger stops. "They're alive in that skull of yours, aren't they? Tony. Bob. And me, I'm young . . ."

He draws his hand away. Jabs his own forehead. The fingernail leaves a deep white crescent in the wrinkled skin. "But the truth is in here."

The hand moves to open a shutter, revealing the frozen lightning brilliance of a million stars.

"Lot of debris. *Volunteers?*"

I flinch at the snap in his voice, more order than request. I know this scene from Jupiter Turnabout by heart: The motors on the main communication antenna have jammed. Now that Tony's fixed the drive, the antenna needs to be freed up to receive vital course data from Earth. But the disaster surrounded the ship with dangerous debris. Bob Winston, a pilot almost as good as Val and one of my favorite crewmembers, volunteers to go out.

". . . he's hit!"

My skin shrinks, remembering the way Bob spun, like a figure skater in a fast twirl, white vapor spiraling around him. A bit of shrapnel no bigger than a fly hit his jet pack, crippled it. Bob's drifted too far from the ship. His oxygen is running out. But he's got just *enough* oxygen. Val jets out to rescue him, heedless of his own danger.

Sunshine flares as the barbecue roll brings the window sunward. We both recoil at the brightness. Slowly, he draws the shutter closed, bows his head.

"If it had been just me and him . . . I'd have risked everything to go after him." He looks at me, raw grief on his face. "Two hundred other people were depending on me. I couldn't . . ."

What's going on in his head? Sounds like he's saying they left Bob out there to die.

"Captain's burden . . ." His voice sinks and roughens, then damps out entirely. His eyes roll white. The lids flutter, then close. He freezes, draped on the air like a puppet suddenly abandoned. The bottle spins above his right hand.

I hug my knees, pull into a small ball. A stink steams off my sweaty skin. It wasn't the way he says. It wasn't.

He twitches, cries out "Harry!" but doesn't wake up. His head wobbles like it's on a spring. His arms float limply. His troubled breathing trembles on the verge of a snore.

Who's Harry? Another imaginary victim of another disaster? If he's going to live in a fantasy, why does it have to be tragic?

The ship shudders as the NavComp automatically fires a thruster to make some microscopic course adjustment.

NavComp!

I unspring. Rise smack into the button-studded ceiling. Grab a handhold and haul myself face-to-face with the mission clock. Did I miss it? I don't remember hearing a prompt. Where's the clipboard? Adrift behind the seats. I snatch it out of the air, quickly scan the mission profile. It's okay, still a few minutes before the maneuver.

None of this commotion has bothered him one bit.

The instruments murmur, shifting and changing. On middeck, the fan in the beat-up environmental unit squeaks rhythmically. Something twangs in the nose of the ship. This tub is like an old house—creaking, settling, slowly falling apart! And outside, pulling at every square inch of the stressed-out old hull, is vacuum and cold and instant death.

Beep.

The sequence matches exactly. I check it off.

"See?" I flash the clipboard at him, but he's oblivious. His body floats against the slack harness, half out of the seat. His arms hang in the air, like someone doing the dead man's float.

What if something went wrong?

Through the gap between his back and the seat, I

see the radio. There's an hour until the next maneuver, then a busy stretch for the rest of the watch. Better do it now. I squeeze into the gap, trying not to touch him. One arm and my head poke out the other side. The radio is only inches from my nose. All the indicators are dark. The power switch . . . locked out! With an old fashioned key-lock!

"I hate you!"

I struggle backward, elbowing his back, thrusting against his ribs. A little grunt escapes him, but that's all. His eyes skim rapidly beneath their lids. Tension draws his mouth flat and thin.

"I don't care who you think you are, mister, you've had your last drunken fantasy!"

I haul myself over the top of the seat, aiming for the hatch to middeck. Hand over hand, I follow the ladder into the chill darkness until my fingers touch the deck. I grope along the wall for the control panel, feel a row of switches, but then draw back. I don't even know which one works the lights!

I take a few deep breaths and wait for my eyes to adjust to the dim light diffusing through the hatch from flight deck. Things take on a gray flatness. I can just make out the labels next to the switches. Click.

A single bulb comes on. The white beam blazes and, as if granting me permission, shines smack on the duffel. I crawl along the wall over to it, unhook the strap, then sail to the toilet. I yank open the zipper. The bottles spill out like seeds from a pod. I snatch one, break the seal, and squeeze. The plastic gives. The whiskey beads at the tip of the straw. Harder. A blob floats free. Just like my tears before, the liquid quivers and undulates as if something inside is pulling it into shape. Then it settles into a perfect amber bubble. Beautiful.

I turn on the toilet—*vrooooommmmm*—and then turn it off again quick. If that doesn't wake him . . . Nothing. On again. I touch the end of the urine tube to the bubble of whiskey. Slllurp!

For a long time, I make bubbles and vacuum them away. When the last bottle is empty, I sweep my gaze over the area to make sure I haven't missed one. The faceted surfaces of the bottles reflect the beam into a hundred snips of rainbow.

The light reflects dully off a flat, square surface— one of the award folders. The tie has loosened and they're drifting around. Maybe the truth is in there.

I snag the nearest folder and spread it open. A silver disc the size of a tea saucer glitters in the recessed velvet pocket. The image embossed on the surface shows Venus in the background, the Lance Ramjet in the middle ground, and an astronaut in the foreground, his helmet tucked in the crook of his arm, his pilot's ponytail curled along the rim of the suit's ringed collar like a pet rat. Words circle the image: Alldrives Pilot Achievement Award • Val Thorsten • First Human Reconnaissance of Venus. Val's first mission for them.

This isn't a fan club replica. It's full-size. The metal is pure titiniamite, I can tell by the feel—same slick iciness as the coating on Dad's space suit. I look toward flight deck. How can he have this? Val wouldn't sell any of his medals. Did this guy steal it? Is that what we're really doing out here—running from the law? But that doesn't make sense. Wouldn't you take on a helper *before* the crime?

Reluctantly, I examine the medal again. The face of the astronaut . . . every detail is microperfect, etched with a laser. It isn't the face of the Val Thorsten I know from thirty-two 3-Vid adventures or from the fan club posters and replica medals—it's the face of the unconscious drunk on flight deck!

I line all the open folders up in midair, every mission from Venus to Neptune. Every face is his face, getting older.

It's true. I'm going to the Moon with Val Thorsten.

MISSION TIME

T plus 14:38:13

A sound, fluttery, like bat's wings. Reflexively, my hand moves to protect my face. I turn my head away from the floating mural of medals toward the sound.

Can't be a bat in here!

Something wrong? Something *ticking*?

Flut flut flut flut flut.

The sound comes from the opposite corner, near the far edge of the lockers, at deck level. I take in a slow breath. It's only the book, the one that was sandwiched between the medals. It's wedged in an air vent. The blowing air is flipping the pages.

Could it be his journal? Maybe it can tell me what happened to bring Val so low. I sure never read anything about it in the official history put out by the fan club.

I kick off and quickly fly across middeck to the

vent. I stick a finger between the pages. Warm air puffs along my forearm. Hooking a floor strap with my foot, I settle into the bubble of warmth near the vent. I smooth the flat of my hand over the page. It's paper! And handwritten! The script is tiny, neat with a spiky edge. The pages are filled with dates and stellar coordinates with an occasional note. It's a log.

May 8, 2153 001 234 999 range sphere B—nothing
May 30, 2153 857 000 419 range sphere W—nothing

Some kind of search, getting nowhere. I flip the page. The only large block of text immediately draws my eye.

July 19, 2153 Bad night. Endless dreams. I relive the preflight walk down. Every bolt, every circuit board, every line of code. What did we miss? I'll go mad! Maybe you already have . . .

Flip.

Fight fight fight, all day, stupid HOOPscope bureaucrats. Finally convinced them to search quadrant seven. Don't know how much longer they'll be bullied . . .

August 4, 2153 quadrant seven—nothing

August 5, 2153 quadrant seven—nothing

Pages filled with that, day by day, until . . .

November 1, 2153 HOOPscope's pulled from search and rescue. Midnight. On the beach. Looking to Cassiopeia. Wondering, where are you? Is the ship holding together? Are you? Beaming love and strength your way, Val.

It isn't his log. It's someone else's, but whose? I hold my place with my finger and turn to the cover. There's no title, no author, just a #5. What's that mean? Slipping my finger out, I open to the first page. A letter on different-colored paper is taped to the inside cover:

Dearest Val,

It's three years since the Valadium Thruster went missing during the Saturn Whip maneuver. Nobody has been able to figure out what went wrong, or if you even survived, and if you did, exactly where the ship might be right now. Certainly, it was no ordinary disaster that ripped the Valadium Thruster from its planned course to Pluto.

This journal is a record of my faith; in our ship, in you. The past three years have yielded enough clues to keep that faith alive. We've glimpsed the ship. We BELIEVE you're alive in it. This details our efforts planetside. We can only guess at the dimensions of your ordeal out there. I hope this fragment of my heart reaches you, so you can know you are always in our thoughts, ceaselessly in our actions, never forgotten.

I've placed a copy of this journal in each lifeboat. I'm so sorry we could only afford six. Peter says that gives us one chance in a billion—fair enough odds for Val Thorsten, huh?

Forgive me, Val, I must move on now.

Love, Maggie

Maggie? Mom's nickname. Is this my mother's journal? What does she have to do with Val Thorsten?

I turn to the first entry: a photocopy of a small scrap of New Frisco General Hospital stationery is glued in. New Frisco General is the hospital *I* was born in. The scrap is dated October 28, 2152—*my* birth date, thirteen years ago. The words are hard to make out, written in a hasty scrawl.

i want to scream! i want to wail! to keen like my irish ancestors used to! but my precious new boy sleeps at my breast. this page must absorb my pain, be a shield for his newness.

The scribbles suddenly get easier to read. The writer's pulled herself under control.

Ted brought the news that something went wrong out near Saturn. Nobody has any details.

Ted—Dad! This *is* Mom's journal! I trace my finger over the close-spaced, spiky writing. Mom's words. No one ever told me she knew Val—or that the Valadium Thruster went missing the day I was born.

Wait a minute. *That's* the anniversary he was talking about! I never bothered to look up the real history. Or maybe I did and the Counselor made me forget. It must have. Otherwise, I have to believe Mom never mentioned Val Thorsten the entire six years we shared, even when she was working so hard on this search.

But if the old spacer *is* Val Thorsten, why didn't *he* tell me he knew Mom? Soon as he learned my full name, he might've guessed I was her son. And if he went to the trouble of finding out my birthday, he definitely found out. So why did he try to send me away when I showed up at the Old Spaceport that second time? Sure sounds like Mom cared about him a lot. Wouldn't he owe it to her to help me?

I feel dazed. Maybe this journal is the way to undo what the Counselor did to me. Mom wrote it for Val to read, but could she have known that someday I would read it, too? I swallow hard and turn the page.

December 14, 2152 Theories abound . . . most conclude you went in over Saturn. There's talk of calling off the search! I won't let that happen. I don't feel you gone from the universe. You pulled her out. I'm sure you did. You always have before. I'm talking to Peter, to Uhura, and our team in India. Hang in there, Val, we'll figure out a way to help you.

For several pages, the entries are sketchy, mostly technical details, with long gaps between. Then there's the section I first opened to, followed by short entries, like weather notes, day after day, page after page. I flip pages fast, scanning for big black blocks of writing.

October 1, 2154 Argued with Ted about how much time I'm spending on this search. He refuses to ac-

cept the need for hurry. The ship had resources enough to keep you alive for years. But what about your mental reserves? Getting to you soon might make all the difference.

October again, but almost two years have passed since the first entry. Did Mom do anything else but work on the search all that time? No wonder Dad was upset. Must've been like having her away on a space mission. He and Mark always told me how lonely they felt without her. Now I feel it, too. She hasn't written one thing about me.

October 16, 2154 Call from an astronomer on Mars, noticed strange spectral shifts 888 514 345 range sphere Z. One of our trajectory plausibles... Could it be the VT drives firing? Must dredge up the strength to force them to do a full HOOPscope survey.

More hopeless search data, then . . .

October 28, 2154 Stewart's second birthday. Ted had to force me to take time to celebrate. Grateful to him, but it was hard. The sphere Z search was ter—

minated today. Hope I'm not putting my family through all this for a dead man.

A little jolt of weirdness comes, like Mom had somehow heard me complain that she never mentioned me. But that entry doesn't exactly leave a happy feeling...

January 20, 2155 Those devils! Alldrives just released Pluto: A Star too Far. They show you home, Val! Rescued! Most of the world thinks you're really back. I know you sold them your "image" to finance the VT, but it's come back to haunt us. They made that 3-Vid to hide something.

February 1, 2155 Donations dropping off even from the hard-core fan clubs. We liquidated Thorsten Engineering to fund Ulura's lifeboat idea. Sad day. Angry day!

Thorsten Engineering. TE. My mind reels back to the moment he gave me those insignias. "Before your time, kid." Val had his own company? I always thought Alldrives built the Valadium Thruster. And what are these lifeboats Mom keeps talking about? I don't remember any lifeboats in Pluto: A Star too Far. Isn't *anything* from the 3-Vids true?

February 18, 2155 I can't do it today, can't work up an image of you alive, moving toward home. So sorry. What could have gone wrong? Did we fail you somehow? The question haunts us . . .

February 19 Big blowup with Ted. I feel sorry for him. He doesn't understand the pure passion that binds us. He still thinks we had an affair during those six months I spent in the asteroid belt with you doing the final systems check of the VT.

Affair? Mom and *him*? Women were always after Val. No. That's the actor, the young and handsome one. This must be about 14 years ago. He'd have been 107 Earth years old; 67 spacer years?—no that's not right, it would depend on what kind of space travel he'd been doing during those years. But he wouldn't have been any *older* than 67.

She wouldn't have . . . would she? Mom was so beautiful. He's so . . . gross. But that long ago he must've been more like the 3-Vid Val, at least in spirit. Lucky Mom, to know him while he was still great.

May 19, 2155 Someone saw the VT! At least, we're pretty sure it was you. This guy reviewing old sur-

very pictures of Andromeda saw a smear. The image is way off the solar plane. Ulura did a spectral and it looks like VT engines. Dovetails with Peter's wildest theories: a transdimensional fold.

Hey! That's my theory!

Now I know why he didn't laugh at me when I suggested it. Because Val Thorsten's the only person in the universe who knows it's true! And if it is true, if a transdimensional shift could be done on purpose, controlled, then someday someone could finally build a star drive!

May 23, 2155 It was you! We have the vector we need. We don't have speed or angular momentum, but at least now there's a chance we can put a lifeboat in your path. I can see you today, working the charts, plotting the way home. Godspeed, Val.

There's that lifeboat idea again.

June 13, 2155 Got Mark into trouble, though nobody knows I put him up to it. They caught him hacking into TLA corporate.

Mark? Our Mark? He'd have been something like nine years old. I scan a line ahead—*Ted really had to pull some strings*—it is Mark. Wow! A hacker genius at nine!

Alldrives didn't waste any time knocking on our door. We did all right making it into a "boys will be boys" thing. They suspect I'm behind it, snooping for something to confirm our growing suspicion about sabotage. Mark played it well, fooled them, thank God he even fooled Ted. The little extortionist, I had to promise to stay planetside a whole year!

November 27, 2155 They're ready—six lifeboats, six of our best trajectory guesstimates. We've calculated what might have run out, what you might need. A pack of cards. A copy of my journal in all of them. Stewart wanted to help. Made the ultimate sacrifice: His Lance Ramjet toy is in #3 —lucky three because he just turned three.

My toy. The memory this morning—no, yesterday now—sunshine and Mom making up some waffles and the long-nosed, fat-engined toy heavy in my hands. Was it only yesterday that I remembered that?

Suddenly more layers come. Without a squiggle, just easy like a normal person might remember: how I puckered my lips to make the spluttery noise of flaming out engines. I never used the batteries. Always made the sound effects myself.

I look at the duffel. I'm about to go check if somehow I missed the toy packed inside, when I realize what #5 on the cover means: This copy of the journal is from lifeboat #5. Number five must be the one that reached the Valadium Thruster. That means lifeboat #3, with my toy in it, is still adrift in deep space, going where no toy has gone before. I read on.

He's one of us, Val. Been fooling around with a little AstroNav, just concepts, you know how you can while tossing a ball. No math yet, of course. Stewart eats it up. He loves Betelguese . . . though that usually ends our lesson in giggles. I'm babbling, a mother's pride. It's pitiful, these little ships, the little we can do. May God grant it's enough.

AstroNav! When I was three years old! The Counselors *did* ruin my skills, just like the old spa—*Val*—warned they could. Why would they do that? This journal isn't going to tell me. It's finished. Last entry. Last page.

One chance in a billion . . . and a lifeboat found him. How long from launch until lifeboat #5 intercepted the Valadium Thruster? I don't know the angles, or the speeds.

Did Mom ever know all her efforts paid off? Did she know Val survived?

Even with so much to jog my memory, there's this vast nothing where the answers should be. I recheck the dates—just over three years since the first entry. Now I'm really confused. In Pluto: A Star too Far, Val was lost for only three years. But according to the journal, after three years, Mom is just sending off the lifeboats.

So when *did* Val really come back? Before or after Mom's crash? I don't know. I don't know the real dates because the 3-Vids faked it and my family kept all this secret from me. Why?

Maybe I missed something in one of the short entries. I need to read every word over again.

14

MISSION TIME

T plus 19:24:14

THE lights come on.

"What the . . . my booze!"

He's halfway down the ladder, feet anchored in a rung, body jutting into middeck. He rips a squeeze bottle out of the air, tilts it against the light to see if even a drop is left. He crushes it. Flings it away. It ricochets off the wall, careens into several others.

He sees me. "You messed with my stuff!"

"You knew my mom!" I hold the journal toward him like a sacred offering. "I want my memories back!"

"I don't care *what* you want! You left your post. You messed with my stuff. I should blow you out the crap dump!"

"It's—"

"Shut up!" The words are twin explosions that

leave my ears ringing. He winces and grabs at his temple, mouth wrenched into an *O* of pain. Headache. He deserves it.

I look hard at him. Nothing in the slatelike planes of his face, the whole ruggedness of him, reminds me of me, but people always say I got a double dose of Mom's genes.

No way I want him to be my father, but he and Mom were in the asteroid belt together the right amount of time before I was born.

He continues in a whisper, each word edged with strangled rage. "Clean this mess. Get in that exercise machine. Put in your hour or so help me . . ."

He takes one more look around. "You're lucky I need you."

A fierce pull on a ladder rung rockets him into flight deck. I hear a thump and a curse. Another thump as he bumps around. Move slow and easy, he told me. I hope he busts something—

Busted.

Like the NavComp.

Suddenly, I realize what I've done. I got so caught up in the journal, I forgot to watch the NavComp!

"It's your fault! You lie like the rest of them!" I soar around scooping up the empty bottles, the awards, the journal; stuff them all back in the duffel.

None of this would be happening if people hadn't lied to me! All those years, worshipping the 3-Vid Val Thorsten while Dad knew. Mark knew. They could've told me the real stories, about Val and Mom working together. Mom must've kept a copy of the journal. They never showed me.

I attack the exercise machine.

Hate him.

Hate Dad.

Hate Mark.

How *could* they do that to me? *Why* would they?

I pound through the routines until all my muscles ache as much as my heart. I stop, sweaty, warm at least, and winded. My breath turns cloudy. It's getting colder in here than it should be. Maybe I messed something up that's causing that. I can't wait an hour to find out.

I slip out of the straps and kick off for the hatch, brake to a stop with the upper half of my body sticking into flight deck.

"Every stinking bottle . . . " he mutters as he consults the three pages of mission profile floating beside him. He doesn't sound very focused.

"Is everything okay?"

He freezes. Sniffs hard. "Something stinks around here."

He grabs a manual, pulls it free with a rip of Velcro. He fires it over his shoulder. "Go change the odor filter."

I catch it: *Commode Operations Manual.* Latrine duty! "You can't bully me."

"I gave you a job. Do it."

"No. I may have left my post, but you were passed out drunk. You might as well have abandoned ship! I *had* to get rid of that stuff."

He twists around to stare at me. His thin lips turn down grimly. His teeth grind once. Make a sound like tectonic plates shifting. He heaves a deep sigh. "You got me talking about my missions, didn't you."

"Don't you remember?"

"I try never to remember . . . but you make it hard, kid. When I look at you, I see Maggie. And when you speak up to me . . . she did that, too."

"Why didn't you tell me you knew her?"

"Secrecy's become a habit and . . . well, I've seen the 3-Vids. Part of me wants to believe my life is still like that."

The best pilot in the universe. The one all the ladies want. "You're my father, aren't you?"

He shakes his head. "That's a load of romantic crap, kid. I didn't think you watched those kind of 3-Vids."

"It's in the journal."

"You didn't read carefully enough! That was all in your father's imagination. I loved Maggie, but never that way. These babies"— he slaps a sidewall strut— "they're my true love, always have been. They're not messy like people. They break down, sure, but it's all in the laws of physics. You can count on it. It's people you gotta watch out for."

"You're telling me!"

He laughs. It's a full, deep sound. I like it.

"Forget the stinking toilet," he says. "Get in your seat."

I thrust out of the hatch, bump off the ceiling, and drop into the copilot seat, hard. I snug up my harness. "So why did you try to send me away?"

"I figured I owed it to Maggie to keep you out of this."

"You were right about the Counselors messing with my head. I don't remember anything about Mom's connection to you. Can you help me get my memories of her back?"

"Lot of memories of Maggie, kid. She was carrying you like a spare oxygen tank when I left for Pluto." He looks away, fixes his eyes on the globe of the astrogator. "I could probably jog something loose in that head of yours. But not now. Not here. The mission—"

"I don't care about your stupid mission."

"You've got to!" He rounds on me and smacks the

center console, making a loud crack of sound. "With all your heart and mind and soul or you're going to die."

"You're going to kill me?"

"Jeez, kid, *I'm* not going to kill you." He checks the timing on the next mission event, then folds the profile and returns it to the clipboard. Just when I think he's giving me the silent treatment, he says, "Answer me this, Mister-I'm-going-to-Pluto. What's the standard ratio of simulator time to actual flight time for a pilot training on an unfamiliar ship?"

His question is straight from the Space Academy exam books. I tell him, "Two hundred to one."

"Right. We're almost at midcourse. In just about nineteen hours, you're going to take a ride in the squid. Have I made my point?"

What have I got so far—four deadly crashes and less than an hour sim-time? "Yeah."

"Good. There's a critical course correction burn coming up in seventy minutes. After that, you're back in the squid." He adjusts a few dials, then snugs up his seat harness. He hits a switch and solitaire comes up on #1 monitor in front of him.

"Hey, I don't get it. You just laid all this heavy stuff on me about sticking to the mission, but you can play games?"

He makes a few bad moves, then switches the

screen off with a strangled growl. He stares at the blackness. "Damn, kid, I could use my booze."

Critical maneuver coming up, he said. I did the right thing dumping that stuff. "You know, I could focus on the mission a lot better if you told me what we're after and what exactly you want *me* to do."

"This mission—" He stops and his jaw works like he's chewing on a tough piece of meat. Is he going to dodge again? "It's revenge, kid. *Justice.* Maggie guessed right—Alldrives sabotaged the Valadium Thruster."

"Sabotaged . . . ?" Alldrives and Val Thorsten are the polestars of my universe. Now he's telling me one of them is a false star. It's hard to swallow.

But Mom suspected Alldrives was involved in the failure of the Pluto mission. She said they faked the *Pluto: A Star Too Far* 3-Vid. If I hadn't read that, I might think he was simply cracked. That he made it up to explain some flaw in the impulsor engines he designed. So he could live with himself.

"What's the Moon got to do with it?"

He answers without any hesitation this time. "The proof I need to finger Alldrives is on the Moon. Hidden. You're going to get it back for me."

"It?"

"The NavComp core from the Valadium Thruster. I ditched it there for safekeeping as I flew by on my way to Earth in the lifeboat. Every line of code in that core is corrupted with Alldrives' unique software signature, damning as a fingerprint."

He unzips yet another pocket in his jacket, reaches in, and takes out a folded paper. Hands it to me. It's yellowed and crinkled and soft as leather. Carefully, I unfold it. It looks like a treasure map. There's a drawing of a square in the center of the paper. Inside that, the coordinates 128 321 004 range sphere M— Tranquility Base! The square must represent the perimeter fence. The southwest post is circled. A line angles 45 degrees from there and ends in an X.

"Now there are two people in the universe who know where that core is hidden, kid." He sounds choked up.

I'm holding something more precious than any of his medals. A piece of his life, he said at the Old Spaceport. Six years lost in space. And then what, another six lost to the booze? "You should've told me right at the beginning. I'd have come in a second to help you."

He shrugs. "Had to be cautious, kid. If Alldrives got the smallest hint of what I'm up to they'd strip mine half the Moon to find that core and destroy it."

The only evidence of what really happened all those years ago in the rings of Saturn, nearly eight hundred million miles away. I fold the map and hand it back to him. He tucks it in the pocket and zips it closed. "Why did they do it, Val?"

"Because it was *my* ship, that's why! I designed her. I raised the capital to build her. I tell ya, kid, the Valadium Thruster really knocked their gyros out of sync at Alldrives. Challenged their supremacy; their wallets; their pride. Old Man Lance, he and I saw eye to eye, had an understanding. But he was long dead when the government put out bids for a Pluto mission. Mr. Lance the Younger . . . what a piece of work. Thought he *owned* me because I let them make those 3-Vids."

"So you went off on your own?"

"Yup. The Younger thought I was just a dumb flyboy—strap a new firecracker to my butt and I'm set to go. But I had a few ideas. When Alldrives wouldn't listen, I started Thorsten Engineering. Put together quite a team. We won the bid for the Pluto mission. Took it away from Alldrives."

"And Mom was part of your team. Tell me more about her."

He shakes his head. "When you get back, after you see the Counselors—"

"What?! You said stay away from them! You said it's good to hang on to memories."

"I'm no model, kid. You've seen that. You're caught in something they created. You'll need their help to come out of it safely."

"You're making me nervous."

"You should be. I'm nervous. The mnemonic suppression technique . . . well, it's only for the worst cases."

"But that's what I don't understand. What could be worse than watching Mom die in a crash?"

"Tell you something that never made it into a 3-Vid—"

He's off on a tangent again, but then, how would he know the answer to my question? He wasn't even on Earth the first six years of my life. He didn't come back until after the crash. By then, the Counselor had already tampered with my memory. Erased huge pieces of my life, including anything Mom might've told me about Val Thorsten. And Dad and Mark were part of it . . .

I've been sabotaged, too. But it couldn't be for the same reason Alldrives tried to kill Val. Dad wouldn't let the Counselor do that to me because he hated me, would he?

15

MISSION TIME
T plus 20:01:15

YOU interested in this, kid?"

"Yeah. Sorry."

"As I was saying, we experimented with mnemonic suppression on a few deep-space missions, to fight the boredom. The idea was to wipe a day's memory of the routine, monotonous stuff. You'd wake up fresh, like the first day out. Only it's not simple to erase a memory. The mind has multiple redundant systems. The technique left . . . ghosts." He's speaking from experience. Of course, Val Thorsten would try it, would test it. Cutting-edge stuff. "People got jumpy. Paranoid. Like they were just a footstep away from another world."

"Squiggly!"

"Huh?"

"That's what I call . . . what happens. Things kind of shimmer and blur, and then it's a different world."

He gives me a long look, then says, "Yeah. Something like that. Can't have you stepping into a different world up here."

"Look who's talking!"

"We're a sorry crew, kid." He looks away. "From here on, both of us have got to stay focused on this mission. Work is the spacer's friend. Never forget that."

Bing bing bing.

Red lights flare across the board, but they make no sense to me. "What's happening?"

"NavComp crash." He kills the alarm and starts tapping keys. He scans the monitors, head moving like a bird pecking at seeds. Row upon row of numbers stream across the screens. A trajectory plot on #1 monitor shows a time-plot of the course we're supposed to be on with a bold white line. Starting about three hours ago, a red line deviates from the white one. It zigzags erratically. A flashing red dot at the end of it indicates our present position. We're way off course!

"That can't be!" he says.

He grabs the sextant, slams open a shutter. The star field out there is familiar to me from the Apollo simulations. I know what stars he's sighting on: Rigel, Altair, and Fomalhaut. The very first navigators, the ancient Sumerians, named those stars thousands of years ago. Greek, Roman, and Arab mariners were guided by them. Columbus sighted on them to find the new world.

Val's been using them to get us to the Moon.

He breezes through the AstroNav calculations to verify our position. I've never seen anyone do AstroNav like that. He makes another calculation, too quick for me to catch the details of his technique. "Show me how you did that."

He shoots me a disgusted look. "Get real, kid, we're in big trouble. If we don't get back on course before midcourse burn is due, we're going to miss the Moon."

"What about the backup system?"

"We're using the backup."

"Can't *you* get us on course?"

"Some things aren't humanly possible." He looks over at me like I'm an idiot. "Course corrections at six thousand miles an hour without a NavComp happens to be one of them."

"Exactly what's wrong with it anyway?"

"Trim your jets." He turns back to the controls. "I was just about to troubleshoot it."

Tap . . . tap . . . tap . . .

He's so slow! I can tell right off he hasn't got any real computer sense—not like Dad or Mark.

"How long until midcourse burn?"

"Forty minutes."

"Forty minutes!" I switch NavComp control to my keyboard.

"Hey, what're you doing?" He reaches over to shut down my terminal.

"Leave me alone." I push his hand away. "I can fly computers!"

First thing is to put the machine through some simple tasks to get an idea if it's a software or hardware problem. If we've got a software problem, we're probably done for.

I tell him to take notes. In a few minutes, I have him read them back to me. I see the problem immediately. "We've got a hardware failure in subsystem A12. Let's open it up."

Together, we unscrew the retaining bolts from the faceplate of the NavComp. I pull the computer out. It's a two-foot cube with hundreds of cables plugged into it. Floating between us, it looks like an upside-down jellyfish.

"Oh God!" he groans, raising his hands in a protective gesture as if it's a *poisonous* jellyfish.

The complexity scares him, but I know this machine—an old model 2X50. Dad was always pushing me into his field. *Away* from Mom. I resented it then, but right now, I'm just glad I paid enough attention to know what to do next.

"Got a test kit?"

He takes a pouch from a locker under the seat. He passes it to me. "You really know what you're doing, kid?"

"I took these apart in my playpen."

He actually smiles. "Okay."

I splice in the test equipment. It doesn't take long to isolate the problem: a black box between the NavComp and the automatic maneuvering system. It converts computer code into electromechanical signals that aim the thrusters. I try a test code. The monitor reads perfect data going in from the NavComp, but the output is total garbage. There's a serious problem in there, all right. It's a sealed unit, meant to be replaced, not repaired.

"It's dead. Got another one?"

I know the answer even before he says, "No. Can't you fix it?"

I poke at the casing with the test probe. "It would take hours just to open it."

He stares at the half globe of the artificial horizon like it was a crystal ball. "Game's up, then."

Just one dead end and he's giving up? There are a dozen options we haven't explored yet. Is he really just going to sit there and let us miss the Moon?

"Val Thorsten never gives up!"

"You're a witness to history, kid. It's over."

Men and women fought for the privilege of shipping out with Val Thorsten. But that's not who I shipped out with. He hasn't got the guts anymore.

"Call for help."

"Huh?"

"Use the radio! Call the Moon. Call Earth! Anybody!"

"You don't understand." He takes a deep breath and presses his head hard into the cushions. His breath wheezes slowly out. "Nobody can reach us in time."

"Of course they can!" Just because he's Val Thorsten doesn't mean he isn't crazy. "We're just going to miss the Moon, not drop off the edge of the universe. Even if we drifted for a week—"

"Don't have a week. Twenty hours, max, we'll be out of air."

"*What?!*"

"There's nothing wrong with the fuel cells, kid. That was just a story to keep you from panicking. It's the oxygen. Most of it vented when we overheated leaving orbit. Discovered it when I had to switch tanks too early."

"You made me exercise!" I can't breathe normally suddenly, even though there's still plenty of air. The fear of running out is like the heavy pressure of liftoff, keeping my lungs from expanding.

"You know what space travel is, kid? It's like trying to skim a stone across a pond. Takes a good ship, a lot of skill, and luck to make it. We just ran out of all three."

"Stop talking like that!" My body says "breathe," but my mind says "hold each breath tight." My chest burns. "You should've turned back!"

"Been an all-or-nothing mission from the first, kid. A final voyage to restore my good name. Not a bad way to go."

"I can't die out here! I need those AstroNav lessons. I need answers."

"I'm sorry, kid. I meant to do you a favor . . . but losing your mother should've taught you. When you reach for the stars, you sometimes get burned."

"No. It taught me to be like you. You always pull it out."

He closes his eyes. He's calm. He looks like a person in church, praying. He hasn't *given* up, he's *choosing* this end.

"Maybe they'll make a 3-Vid. Val Thorsten's Final Voyage. Leave out the stink. Put us in one of those spiffy Comet Catchers. We'll live, of course."

"We'll live now!" I attack the controls like a fool, throwing switches, setting knobs, punching in parameters, hoping to make him so nervous he'll help.

His eyes stay closed. I'll have to pull this out myself.

More calmly, I really try to set a course for this tub. Bad as I am at AstroNav, I can still tell that it doesn't look good.

I notice a bank of knobs off to my left. The nameplate reads: MANEUVERING THRUSTER ALIGNMENT— MANUAL CONTROL SYSTEM.

Manual. For people. It's what the broken black box did automatically.

"Hey! Hey!" I reach around the dangling NavComp and shake him hard. It takes forever for his eyes to open and focus on me. "We don't need that stupid black box!"

"Huh?"

"We need a *pilot*! Look!" I point at the matching manual thruster controls on his side. His gaze kind of drifts that way, but he stays slouched in the seat. "Don't you understand? The NavComp is giving good data! You can read the code and fire the thrusters manually."

He twists away so I'm looking at his back. He doesn't want to hear my idea. He doesn't want to get out of this.

"You *can* fly this tub, can't you?"

"Stupid kid," he mutters to the window. I strain to hear. "There are thirty thrusters on this thing. Damn PLV only had five. Barely handled that."

"I don't care! You're Val Thorsten. You've got to try!" Rage fuels my arm muscle. I punch him, the force lost in the heavy jacket. Quick as ever, he catches my wrist. Holds it in iron. My eyes tear, blurring his old face. "Please . . . be Val Thorsten. We need him."

I smear the tears away in time to see him glance at the manual controls. His gaze jumps away. Can't blame him. The thruster controls cover a couple of feet of panel; thirty boxes with dials, knobs, and switches. No one could handle so many. Not alone.

"What if I read the code and set the thrusters? You fire them and the main engines. Won't that work?"

"Look, kid. Look!" He pushes his other hand into the tangle of wires. The fingers tremble like an insect struggling in a spider's web.

"So what? You docked us and kept us from blowing up!"

He makes a fist. His jaw muscles tighten.

"You know why you've always been my hero?"

His eyes narrow.

"Because I've known . . . ever since the crash . . . deep in my heart, I just know if you'd been the pilot of that shuttle, Mom would be alive today. Val Thorsten always brings home the crew."

"Damn . . ." His eyes squeeze shut, hard, for so long

that I worry I've lost him again. Then he shakes his head like he's waking from a bad dream. "Can you really rig it like you said, dual control?"

"You bet!"

"Okay. Do it." He releases my arm.

I give it a victory pump. "Yeah!"

"One thing, kid."

"What?"

"It was only the ship."

"What do you mean?"

"Val Thorsten always brought home the ship."

16

MISSION TIME

T plus 20:28:16

BY the time I'm done making the adjustments, there are only twenty minutes left until the mid-course burn.

He locks in the coordinates. "All set?"

I can only nod. My eyes are locked on the thirty small thruster control boxes that are my responsibility. For each manuever, I have to pick the right box and set its controls faster than I've ever done anything before.

"Watch that screen." He activates the NavComp, which begins the complex calculations.

I force my eyes away from the boxes to focus on #2 monitor. It's blank. Any moment, the first thruster code could come up. But the seconds drag. The screen stays blank. It's weird, a computer taking so long, but

I had to slow it down to human speed. We'd never be able to keep pace with it otherwise.

I steal a glance at him. He's hunched forward. Sweat beads along the sides of his neck. His knuckles are white from gripping the joystick. His other fingers tap anxiously near the fire control button.

His job is to fire the thruster for the correct burn duration, then work the compensators to prevent any overcorrection of our course. And then there's the midcourse burn using the main engines. That he has to do alone.

Unless he falls apart . . .

He catches my anxious look.

"The screen." He points. I snap my head back. Still blank. "We take it one step at a time, kid. Forget the last move, don't think about the next one. Become those thruster controls."

The code flashes—AV-7 Yaw 78 Pitch 03 Roll 00—frighteningly white and huge on the black screen. I find thruster AV-7, twist the knob, punch the buttons, flip the switches. Tell him, "Set!"

The shuttle shudders once, then three more times as he works the compensators to settle us on the new trajectory.

Another code. Locate. Twist, punch, flip. "Set!"

He does his part: two blasts this time, then five with the compensator.

Code.

It goes on and on with barely time for a breath between maneuvers. I glance at #1 monitor. A white line marks the course we need to be on. A red line shows our error. The gap is beginning to close between them. Unfortunately, the nearer we get to a perfect match, the harder it is to bring the two lines together, and the faster the codes come, almost faster than I can set switches.

We start zigzagging across the white line.

A warning sounds.

MIDCOURSE BURN T MINUS FIVE MINUTES.

My eyes blur. I miss a code. Then I set the wrong thruster. I try to correct my mistake, but he's already fired the thruster. It nudges us the wrong way, further off course.

Code comes up to correct my first mistake, then another one before I can even set the switches.

"Don't fire! I missed one!" Another. And now I'm three behind. We'll never make it. I'm blowing it. "I can't do it!"

"Not your fault," he says and shuts down the NavComp. Less than four minutes. We're doomed . . .

"The roll," he says. "Mistake." A series of rapid thruster shots follow his words.

The barbecue roll! The spin on the ship is making the maneuvers too complex. The NavComp can easily handle that kind of complexity because of how fast a computer works. But we both forgot the spin would make our job a thousand times harder at a human pace. It's not easy to think of every detail in a crisis, but a mistake this bad will be hard to recover from. Can he pull us out?

Strain shows in every line of his body as he struggles to stop the spin. His hands are like separate creatures, graceful and sure as they work the joystick. It's beautiful.

"Start again." He turns on the NavComp.

Code. Locate twist punch flip. "Set!"

Two minutes.

Code.

Code.

Code.

The white line flashes red. "On course!"

MIDCOURSE BURN T MINUS ONE MINUTE.

He flips the shuttle to point the engines at the Moon so the thrust will slow our fall into its gravity well. The midcourse burn is all up to him. He scrambles to set switches, running on instinct. There's no time to follow elaborate checklists. "Listen, kid. This'll be a twenty-second burn. Gonna be rough. I can't do it and the thrusters, too. So if a code comes up, you have to make the maneuver. Fail and we're dead."

He reaches over and activates the joystick control on the arm of my seat. I stare at the stick as the meaning of his words sinks in. The moment has come. I get to fly this thing, too!

The turbo pumps growl up to speed. A terrible rattle vibrates through the shuttle. Ignition. Deceleration hits, slamming me into the seat. My arms drop into my lap. As the engines belch to full throttle, blackness sneaks in at the edges of my sight.

A squiggly? A memory? I don't want either one right now!

The engines hiccup, bucking the shuttle violently. A movement catches my eye. His free hand rakes over the controls in a desperate attempt to damp out the rough running. The building acceleration threatens to pull me into unconsciouness. I fight it. Gotta stay focused . . .

"Code!" His urgent voice is a light in the darkness. "Kid, we're drifting!"

Can't drift. We'll miss the Moon. I reach for the thruster control boxes. I'm in a swift stream, fighting a strong current. Time's running out . . . I throw my body forward, grab the edge of the console, and get my fingers on the buttons: twist punch flip to lock in the maneuver.

The code starts flashing. It's the warning sign that I have only a few seconds to make the maneuver or we'll be off course when he makes the burn—disaster!

I fall back. My hand finds the joystick and my thumb squeezes down on the "fire" button at the same instant. I can't feel the punch of the thruster, but the monitor says it fired.

"Compensate. *NOW!*" A voice that hundreds obeyed. A man they *wanted* to obey.

This is the hard part. The NavComp is operating so slowly now it won't be able to tell me how to stabilize the shuttle until it's too late. It's up to me to make the right maneuver. The first time I've touched the controls of this tub. The first and—if I screw up—final test of my skill.

The stuttering roar, the vibration, Val's desperate struggle with the engines—all those worries fade into the only important details I need to know to keep this thing on course: pitch, roll, yaw.

My fingers tighten on the joystick. I make my maneuver.

The main engines go silent . . . end of burn.

Pressure ceases. I come out of my intense focus on my flight panel and see him staring at #1 monitor. I stare, too. It's a perfect white on red match. We're headed to the Moon again.

"We did it," he whispers. His voice grows stronger, louder. "We did it!"

He whoops and shakes my shoulder. He's grinning like crazy. I wonder how his dry old skin can stretch so much without cracking.

"Damn good piloting, kid! Damn good!"

A huge grin pushes at my own ears. I really flew this thing! I kept us on course. I made his struggle with the engines worth it.

My fingers curl lightly around the joystick. A stillness spreads through me. It's really possible now. Stewart Hale ... graduating Space Academy ... first assignment, navigator on the never before attempted—

The clunky old control panels of *Old Glory* blur around me. For a second, I believe it's the force of my own imagination making that happen, but then the air folds, shimmers, and I realize it's a squiggly. The squiggly drops me in front of the sleek, gleaming flight controls of an ultramodern shuttle ...

I'm in the pilot's seat. A little kid. The foot pedals are far from my dangling feet. I admire my silvery gripper booties. Kick them in joy.

"I'm flying to Mars!"

A big, hairy hand closes over mine, gently tries to tug it off the joystick. I look up at Commander Derrick, who's smiling down at me.

"Got to have my seat back now, son."

"No! Let me!"

A gust of laughter from behind the high back of the pilot's seat. Many voices mingle. One special voice . . .

"Mommy?"

I turn to look . . .

. . . and find myself back on *Old Glory* on my knees, turned backward, clinging to the high back of the copilot's seat like a bit of wreckage at sea. Nothing behind us but gutted controls. Dimness. Stink and cold. The beautiful ship is gone.

"What's the matter?" Val twists around to look behind us, too.

"I . . . I thought . . . I heard . . . Mom's voice."

Val mutters, "Ghosts."

I turn my head and meet his narrowed, nervous eyes. He licks his lips. "Get in the squid. We'll train."

17

MISSION TIME
T plus 26:25:17

OKAY, that's enough." The small speaker in the squid makes Val's voice sound tinny and distant. He's coaching me from flight deck so he can make course corrections whenever codes come up.

The simulator screen flickers, goes black. Images of the lunar landscape return every time I blink my eyes. I've been crammed in the squid since we got back on course—hours ago. Every part of my body is numb. I can barely move my left hand anymore. After the first few successful landings, he made me put on the space suit gloves. Every move is like squeezing a rubber ball. It's a real good thing we switched the joystick to my left hand. My right would never have been able to take the strain.

I made a dozen perfect landings in twenty tries. Val said I beat the odds a few times by getting out of some of the wild glitches he threw at me. I'm too exhausted to feel excited anymore. I never want to see Moon craters again!

Well, just once more. Real ones.

There's been no time to think or sort things out, just like in Jupiter Turnabout. Val bullied the crew with regulations, drills, cleanup, and maintenance. Everything by the book and to the letter. They never had a minute to worry about what would happen if the boomerang maneuver failed.

There's this super funny scene where Val badgers Tony to black his boots, again, and Tony says, "Okay, if make-work is what you want, I'll help." He pulls off his boots and socks and puts the polish on his feet. Then he goes dancing all over the ship.

Only, that can't have happened . . .

Keep busy!

I twist out of the squid. It's dark in the canister—more power conservation. Goose bumps pop up as the cold air sucks away my body heat. Usually the problem is keeping a spaceship from getting too hot inside. But with so many systems shut down, there's too little waste heat being generated to keep the temperature anywhere near comfortable. We're running with just one fuel cell to save as much oxygen for breathing as possible.

Following the dim glow from a guide strip, I slip

feetfirst into the narrow tunnel, hook a foothold, then haul the canister hatch shut. In the air lock, I strip off the gloves and clip them on the suit. I shake out the numbness, then close the tunnel hatch to the canister before pushing off into the blackness of middeck. It's cold, refrigerator cold. I pause to close the last hatch. The cold and the clang of the hatch make me think of old submarine movies, of sinking to the bottom of the sea.

Busy doesn't always work!

It's warmer on flight deck, but even here all the lights are off except for two shining on the controls. Val's snug in his jacket. He's squeezing green Gunk— spacer survival rations, officially—into his mouth. My nose wrinkles at the chalky smell of the Gunk as I settle into my seat. Close up, I notice he's shaved.

"Want some?" The words bubble through the paste.

I shake my head. "Makes me gag."

"Drink this anyway. It's loaded with electrolytes and minerals." He hands me some Squirt, then taps his clipboard. "A little surprise—don't look like that, it's a good one for once. I finished analyzing that burn. We shaved nearly six hours off our ETA."

No wonder he was pushing me so hard in the squid. We had planned on one more training session. Twelve out of twenty doesn't seem so good anymore.

I finish sucking down the Squirt. Tastes straight from a chemistry lab. I buckle up. The shifting colors on the instrument panel blur. I force my eyes open. Try to stifle a yawn.

"Go ahead, sleep. I'll take the first watch."

"Don't want to."

"Been there, kid." He washes a mouthful of Gunk down, makes a face at the Squirt. "Too bad you dumped all the booze."

"That wouldn't do *me* any good!"

"Then you'll have to play solitaire." He reaches over and taps a button on my keypad. The game flashes onto #3 monitor on my flight panel. Above the slots for aces is a number: 871,023.

I touch my finger over it. "What's that?"

"Lifetime total games played. I racked up two hundred thousand on the VT alone." He sucks a bit of Gunk from between his teeth.

"If I played that many games, I'd go—"

"Crazy. Yeah. I thought I could handle anything space handed me, kid. I'd been to Mercury alone. Two years no problem. But *six* years!"

"Alone?" I can't be hearing right. Val shipped out with the same old crew in Pluto: A Star Too Far.

"You've got to shake those 3-Vids out of your head. Look." Val clicks a few keys and #2 monitor displays the technical drawings of the Valadium Thruster. Val zeroes in on the crew section, a tiny part of the half-mile long ship. Definitely not big enough for all the people who were in the 3-Vid.

Mom never mentioned anyone else in her journal, either. I pull my knees up and twist in the seat to face him. With my heels wedged against the center console, the position is uncomfortable enough to keep me awake. "It could hold a few people. Why'd you go alone?"

"She was my ship, my design. I believed in her, but after the Jupiter disaster . . . well, I didn't want anyone else to take that risk." He frowns. "As it turned out, a little company would've been welcome."

"Tell me about it."

"Why not?" Val squares his shoulders like a boxer about to step into the ring. "Everything went by the book until the Saturn Whip. The ship was falling into the gravity well, building speed for the final boost to Pluto. Every second I set a new speed record for a human being. Stretched the computers to the limit."

A code flashes. He deals with it almost without looking.

"Just like that!" He snaps his fingers. "She died—*everything!* Then the power came back. And the main drives. They weren't supposed to be on. The controls wouldn't respond. I don't mind saying I panicked, kid, but then it happened, and I was too amazed to be terrified. The bulkheads faded away around me. My body expanded, thinned. It seemed as if solar systems were pushing in between my very cells, until I stood with one foot on Saturn and the other on some star at the other side of the galaxy. Maybe the ship was crashing. Maybe it had exploded. Maybe I was dead. I could've cared less. I felt this joy as I stood there astride the stars . . ."

Hushed, I say, "The transdimensional shift."

He nods. "Then I blacked out. When I came to, everything was solid again and the ship was on her way to Andromeda at full thrust. There wasn't a thing I could do about it. The entire disaster had been programmed into the NavComp."

"Alldrives . . ."

"To punish me. They could've thrown her into Saturn. Killed me outright. Instead, they left me alive and lost forever in space. At least, they thought they had." He opens a shutter, and it's like letting in a winter's night. Andromeda Galaxy glitters, over two million light-years away. "I tell you, kid, the memory of that joy got me through a lot of bad days."

I hug myself. "How were you able to get back?"

"Killed her, system by system. Took a week to get to the reaction chamber and shut down the drive. I purged every system of their treachery, then I brought her back to life. That took a few months. She was mine again, under *my* control. By then, we were way off the plane of the solar system. The Sun was a pinprick of light behind us."

Another code flashes. He doesn't respond. I take care of it. The brief jolt starts him talking again.

"There were only two systems I couldn't repair: the NavComp and the radio-link to Earth."

NavComp crash. Just like what happened to us.

"So that's why you froze when ours went down."

"Yeah."

Our eyes meet. He survived that crisis alone on the Valadium Thruster, but without my help, he would've died out here. The moment is too full of strong feelings. I look away, fix my eyes on that huge number above the aces. "How *did* you make it through?"

"Did I make it? Look at me . . . us . . . now . . . this tub." He waves it all away, mouth set grimly with unhappiness.

I try to think of something to cheer him up. "When did you make contact with the lifeboat?"

"You can't imagine what it meant to pick up that blip." His expression softens. "Your mom was something else, kid."

"Did she know you made it back?"

"The radio in the lifeboat linked on a secret frequency straight to Maggie. We knew Alldrives would do anything to prevent the truth from being known.

We made a plan to hide everything. Get me home quietly as possible. In my condition . . . they'd have chewed me up." Val pauses, then seems to realize he hasn't answered my question. "I was still six months out when she stopped talking to me."

She knew he was alive, knew her efforts had made a difference. She *talked* to him. That's something, even if she was gone when he finally got to Earth.

"Six months at full thrust—" He rakes his hands from temples to jaw. He presses them there, holding himself together. "Burn as long as I could stand it, recover, burn again. Every day . . . every day . . ."

"Full thrust! For months!"

"You've suffered a little in this tub, huh?" He takes his hands away, snorts dismissively. "Bottle rockets compared to what pushed the Valadium Thruster."

"Why'd you stay with the VT when you had the lifeboat?"

"Like I said before, kid. I always bring home the ship. And in this case, it was the evidence against Alldrives. I had to bring it back. For Maggie and the others. Vindicate them. Redeem their years of work. Pilot needs a good team, kid. Never forget that."

"But you don't have one for this mission."

"I didn't before. Now I do."

Part of his team, like Mom. "Why aren't Peter or Ulura helping you get the NavComp core back?"

"That was a dark time, kid." He switches the solitaire to his monitor. Starts a game.

What could have happened to leave him all alone? I know better than to try and push him for an answer. He'd be reaching for a bottle if I hadn't dumped them.

After one rapid click through the pack, he stops. He missed several moves. Staring at the screen, he says with sudden intensity, "You've got to understand, kid. I was half-crazy by then. Maggie's voice was the first live voice I'd heard in years. We set it all up, then she stopped talking to me—"

"The crash."

"Yeah, she was dead. But I didn't know about that! I worried she betrayed me. Can you believe it! When I finally learned what happened, I convinced myself Alldrives had killed her! I knew they would kill anyone who tried to help me."

"But they couldn't . . . wouldn't . . . all those people—to kill my mother? It's not true, is it?"

"No, it isn't. But I believed it. I couldn't involve any of my friends with stakes like that. Tried to settle everything with Lance the Younger, man-to-man."

"Single-handed?!" That sounds like Val Thorsten!

"Yeah. Big mistake. He isn't a man, kid. He's part of this . . . power." He fumbles in his jacket pocket for a bottle. Must be a bad, bad memory. He notices what he's doing, forces his hands flat and still against the flight console. "Took a long time to crawl back into the light. When you bring that core up from the Moon, there'll be hell to pay!"

Fierce. Confident. Here's the Val Thorsten spacers fought to ship out with. That Mom worked so hard for.

"You can count on me, Val." I shiver with excitement.

He mistakes it for the cold. "It'll get colder still."

He reaches under his seat, draws out a blanket. He spreads it over me, tucking the edges in tight.

"Sleep. Dream sweet dreams of revenge." He calls up a new game, glances at me. Winks. "That's an order, kid."

18

MISSION TIME

T plus 38:04:18

NEAR the end of my watch, the light level on flight deck takes a sudden jump. I look out the window. It's the Moon!

"Val! Val!" I shake him. "Val, we're here!"

Which is a stupid thing to say because we're really a couple thousand miles away. Val's sure to yell at me for waking him up. Why would he even care? He's been to nearly every planet, seen a dozen moons.

He struggles awake. One hand rubs at the sand in his eyes while his other hand fumbles with the harness buckle. Then he's free and sliding open a shutter. He puts his face close to the window. For a long time, we both stare.

Copernicus Crater is dead ahead. The crater-roughened and mountain-heaved areas are surrounded by huge patches of smooth surface that look like water. That's why they were given names like Ocean of Storms, Seething Bay, and Sea of Tranquility.

These flat plains are dark. Everything else is the color of a wasp's nest. Dustings of glowing silver grace the rims of the craters. We'll probably skim right over Luna Base before making the burn for orbital insertion. Too bad Dad isn't there to watch.

Something glints where the sharply defined horizon of the Moon meets black space. It could be a ship in orbit, or even the Telecomsat that Dad came here to fix. A tiny speck breaks free of the glittering object and glides toward the surface. A couple more objects flare into view as they swing around from the far side. One is big enough to show some detail. It's a long chain of ore barges from the asteroid belt.

Val grunts. "Crowded."

I laugh because it's crazy. Just three sightings over all the enormous sky of the Moon. But I feel the same way. I liked having the whole universe to ourselves.

An elbow bumps me as Val reaches inside his jacket. He pulls out a key. "LunaCom is going to want to talk to me." He slips the key into the lock on the radio power switch. Pauses. "You with me kid? One hundred percent?"

I bite my lip. He's worried I'll call out for help when he opens the channel. Not long ago, I would have. Might still be the smart thing to do. I don't want to lie to him, so I say, "Ninety-five percent."

"Honest. I like that." He smiles. "You won't mind waiting below while I get us squared away for orbit?"

"No, sir. On my way." The harness releases with a snap and I kick toward the ceiling, tap it, altering my angle and momentum, and do a backflip over the seat. My stomach gently grazes the side wall before I twist and drop through the hatch. Soon as I'm out of sight, I grab a ladder rung, flip, and drift up close to the opening. I just gotta know how he pulls this off!

"*Old Glory* to LunaCom, come in." There's a burst of static and squealing hiss. I peek. He's twisting knobs to make the radio squawk like that. "I say again, LunaCom this is *Old Glory*, do you copy?"

"Barely, *Old Glory*." The voice from LunaCom flight control is perfectly clear on our end. "You copy us?"

"Minimal," he lies and makes a big raspberry. "Got a VHF seven failure. Best I can do. Got CBH long-range telemetry out, too." Squeal. "She's a bucket of bolts, but I love her."

He's sly. Those particular system failures would make any ship practically untrackable.

"Ah, roger that *Old Glory*. Explains why we've had trouble verifying your approach. Are you still on flight path from asteroid field Beta Seven? Over."

LunaCom thinks we're coming in from the asteroid belt! Now I remember. Just after declaring us dead in the capsule burn up, he said something about nobody being able to track us because we weren't coming from Earth. He must have filed a false flight plan.

"Affirmative. Request permission for lunar orbit insertion according to prefiled mission plan."

"Roger that, *Old Glory*. LOI is go. Enjoy the view. And we just have to say, old man, there's more than one screw loose on that ship. LunaCom out."

"Eat your heart out," Val says, wrenching a final eruption of noise from the radio before shutting it off.

I poke my head up. "Wow!"

"Get up here." He motions with his head and, as I settle in, smiles. "Pretty good, huh? They think I'm on a nostalgia cruise—you know, a crazy old spacer who can remember when ships like *Old Glory* were the Comet Catchers of every kid's dream."

I needle him. "Can you really remember that?"

"Thanks, kid. Now shut up. It's time for pitchover."

He works the joystick to rotate the shuttle nose over tail. The Moon slowly slides out of view as our rockets come around to point at it. When the angles are exactly right, he stabilizes us, then shifts right into setting up the burn. Not a motion wasted. He's the pilot of a shuttle preparing for an extremely important maneuver. Nothing else matters anymore. In two minutes, the engine will fire to put us into orbit.

Then *I'm* going to land on the Moon! Not like a tourist coming down in a liner so big and comfortable you might as well be landing anywhere on Earth, but in a miniature LEM, just like the first astronauts.

My excitement somersaults. A big lump sticks in my throat. My eyes water. The cockpit light refracts around Val. For a second, his image blurs. He's the Val Thorsten of Jupiter Turnabout. He's got the old stuff back again. He'll bring me down safe.

Why isn't someone filming now?

"Perfect." He slaps the seat arm. "Time to suit up."

He flows over the seat back, his big body arched like a breaching whale. A tight tuck and roll, then he kicks off the ceiling to plunge through the floor hatch.

I catch up with him in the air lock chamber. He's holding the undergarment of the space suit. It looks like thermal underwear, only it's made to keep you cool. Without that cooling system, a person would stew in their own body heat inside the superinsulated suit.

"Remember, once you're down, you've got to work fast," Val says as I strip. My pants and shirt keep their shape, like in cartoons where the clothes are so dirty they stand up by themselves. "It'll only take twenty-four minutes for a park ranger to arrive once they get suspicious of us."

I nod, slipping a leg into the undergarment. Balancing on one leg is hard on Earth, impossible in outer space. Gravity doesn't hold you to the floor. I start spinning. Val, who's always well anchored, stops me. I use him for a post, slip my other leg in, then my arms, and zip it up. Same procedure with the lower half of the space suit. He helps me with the boots.

I feel like a kid being stuffed into a snowsuit.

Val snugs the Snoopy cap on my head. The cap has a small microphone attached to it by a slender wire and earphones sewn into the sides. Last comes the helmet. He pokes a button on the chest plate and the suit pressurizes. I'm breathing the sweetest air since leaving the PLV. And I'm warm.

He clips the locator to my wrist. I'll use that to find where the bore tube containing the NavComp is drilled into the surface somewhere just outside the perimeter fence. He puts a Snoopy cap on. My earphones hiss. "All right in there?"

I nod.

He squints into the shaded helmet visor and grumbles, "Use your mike."

I dip my chin to enable "talk" and say, "Okay."

"Come on, then."

The suit's too bulky to let me crawl through the

tunnel. I hold my arms out in a *V* and use my toes to nudge along behind Val. The squid looks tiny in the giant cylinder. Perched on the boom, it's silent and fragile seeming, like a Chinese box kite.

At the console, Val makes the final adjustments to the remote telemetry link. "Climb aboard."

I face the opening in the side. This is it. When I crawl in, it won't be for a simulator run. The readings will be real. The alarms will be real. And if something does go wrong, if I have to fly this thing, I'll find out if I've got what it takes to be like Val. Or if I'll fail, like Mom did.

I grip the edge of the opening to pull myself in.

"Hold it." Val stops me. "She needs a name. Bad luck to fly a ship without a name."

"It's been the *Squid* to me since I first saw it."

"No points for creativity, kid." Val takes a marker from his pocket and scrawls SQUID beneath the window. He draws squiggly lines trailing from the letters, like tentacles. "Okay, get in."

I grip the edge again. Immediately, I sense a difference. Naming it has created something personal between the *Squid* and me. I wish suddenly that Val would let me fly her.

I pull. Thunk! The backpack catches on the edge of the opening. Val grips my calves. A tug down, a twist, then he jams me in. My shoulders come up against the padded restraints below the nose window. My feet settle on the curved top of the ascent stage fuel tank. This tank is separate from the one for the descent stage motor. It holds enough fuel to get me back to the shuttle, or, if anything goes wrong with the rocket, to become my own personal land mine.

I squirm to settle in better. My right hand comes down on the keypad. My left finds the joystick. It's such a tight fit, only my head and hands are free to move. "How am I going to get out?"

"Don't worry, there's gravity down there." Val floats in front of the window. A disgusting sound warbles in the earphones, then *Ptaa!*

He spit on my ship! "Hey, what're you doing?"

"Christening her. We're all out of the traditional stuff. Bon voyage, kid." He gives a thumbs-up signal, then starts to turn away.

"Val!"

He pulls up short, presses his face close. "Yeah?"

"Can the Counselor bring the memories back?"

"Focus on the job at hand, kid." Val looks stern. "It's what Maggie did. It's what we all do."

"I'll try, Val."

"Not good enough. Do it. Understood?"

"Yes, sir."

MISSION TIME

T plus 39:09:19

A few minutes pass before the earphones in the Snoopy cap hiss to life. Val's back on flight deck. He says, "Power up checklist. Confirm status green for me."

We work through the list smoothly, not like that first time in orbit around Earth preparing for translunar injection.

"I'm going to blow the lid. One minute." His voice comes crisply over the headphones, but a different whispery soft voice, much more official sounding, echoes in my head.

"Tower Control to FSF Seven Eight, you're go for deorbital burn."

My heart thumps hard. The scar throbs. That's Mom's flight signature!

The *Squid* comes to life. The miniature readouts

framing the window flash through a systems check. Rattled by that echo, the rapidly changing displays mean nothing to me. My guts clench like that time waiting in the wings at the school play—my cue was coming up, but I couldn't remember a single line!

The earphones crackle. "Here we go!"

Hundreds of tiny explosive charges blow the top off the canister. The moisture in the air crystallizes, surrounding me in a glittering fog that immediately whisks out into space.

The shuttle orbits upside down with the *Squid* riding like a bomb in a bomb bay. I'm looking straight down at the surface of the Moon and my arms instinctively try to jerk up to brace for a fall. But they're pinned at my sides over the control boxes. Sharply slanting sunlight makes inky pools of shadow in the craters. Goose bumps erupt all over me.

A thruster blasts and a sharp punch shakes the *Squid.* A quick surge of acceleration pushes my small ship out of the canister. The walls slide away. Black infinity slams into place around me.

Val says, "You're clear of the ship. DOI in sixty seconds."

But that other voice is in my head again, shadowing his words: *"DOI looking good . . . on our way home, folks."*

"Not home," I tell the confused voice. "The Moon."

"Huh?" Val says. "What's that, kid?"

"Nothing." That wasn't Val's voice! Another voice. Another ship. A different announcement of descent orbit initiation. It wasn't a squiggle though. My view of the Moon; the controls of the *Squid*; everything stayed perfectly clear.

A memory . . .?

"Fifteen seconds until DOI," Val says.

Memory or not, I can't afford to listen now! I force myself to focus on the readouts. The *Squid* is seventy miles above the Moon with an orbital velocity of thirty-seven hundred miles per hour.

"Three . . . two . . . one . . . go."

I feel a light push against the soles of my feet. There's no rattle and bump like on the shuttle. The thrust from the *Squid*'s tiny descent engine never reaches an uncomfortable level. The push ends in twenty seconds. The landing radar shows a slight bend in the orbital path. The altimeter reading drops . . . slow and steady.

"Looking good," Val says.

"Sure is."

There's nothing to do until perilune, the lowest point in the new orbit, eight miles up. There isn't even much to look at. The *Squid* flies feetfirst with the window aimed at the stars. It'll pitchover into touchdown position at five thousand feet above the surface.

That's when I might have to fly it, but only if the landing site is too rough for Val to deal with from above.

"Hey, Val."

"Yeah?"

"I'm probably the first person to go down to the Moon in a ship this tiny in years."

"Decades."

"Really?"

"Hold the chatter." The line goes silent. The displays flash a systems check. Then another one.

"What's wrong?" A biological alarm goes off along my nerves. Sweat moistens my skin. Heat flares all over my body.

"Little glitch," Val says. "Just breathe easy, kid, I'm switching to secondary control."

"We're in for a little turbulence folks, nothing to be alarmed about," the whisper says, calm and professional.

That's not Val talking. There can't be turbulence—there's no air on the Moon!

Something's happening to me. It's like my brain has turned into a black box just like the broken one in the NavComp. Val's words make sense going in, then become totally garbled. Except that whispery voice seems familiar somehow . . .

"That did the trick," Val says. "You showing green?"

I sweep my gaze over the tiny instrument panel rimming the nose window. "All green here."

"Okay. Powered descent one minute."

Somewhere, things aren't green. *Something* is going to happen. Something always *does* happen in 3-Vids, because disaster and close calls and steady-in-the-face-of-danger is what they're all about.

"Mark. PDI is go," Val says and the rocket fires. The floor nudges my feet as the thrust gauge leaps, sliding quickly to one hundred percent. Forward speed slows. The Moon tugs. The altimeter starts dropping in one-hundred-foot intervals, nearly a mile a minute. Exactly according to the flight plan.

"Right down U.S. One!" Val says.

U.S. 1 was a famous highway back when there were automobiles. The astronauts named the approach to Tranquility Base after it. We're reenacting the very first Moon landing!

"Approaching pitchover. On my mark . . ."

This is the most critical maneuver next to landing. My grip tightens on the joystick. I limber up the fingers on my right hand, ignoring the stabs of pain as the scar flexes. I lightly touch the keys, reviewing each position and its function. I've got to be ready to take over if anything goes wrong.

"Mark."

A thruster pops. The horizon of the Moon comes into view. Another pop. The *Squid* whirls around until I'm looking along my line of motion. For an instant— then the horizon tilts. The thruster hasn't shut off like it was supposed to! It knocks the *Squid* off course. Forces it into a downward spiral. Starts it spinning like a top. The view through the window goes crazy, flickering intense white from the surface, then the blackest black of space. Suddenly, the world turns Technicolor and I'm not crash diving at the Moon anymore . . .

I'm next to Mom in a seat on Frisco Shuttle Flight 78, crashing. Terror holds my eyes on the dizzying scene out the window as the shuttle rolls over and over again.

Clouds. Now blue ocean. A slice of horizon. Blue-black sky. Flare of sun. Clouds again.

Tumble tumble tumble.

I feel sick, like when I ate too much cake at my birthday. Mom got mad at the mess. So I don't want to get sick. Some people are. I can smell it.

I'm about to make Mom mad at me when the tumble stops.

We're hanging upside down. The seat harness hurts my shoulders. Some people fall onto the ceiling. They're crying. A man is screaming.

"You okay, honey?" Mom asks.

"You're squeezing too hard." Mom lets go of my hand and suddenly she seems far away even though we're hanging upside down right next to each other.

"Commander Hale to flight deck. Commander Hale to flight deck."

That's Commander Derrick calling for Mom. He sounds all funny, like he ate hot peppers. He needs some water. Mom and I visited him earlier in the flight. I sat in the pilot's seat. Then he had to fire the big engines to take us out of orbit. Mom laughed when I wanted to do it.

Good thing we're strapped in or we'd be on the ceiling now, too. Only Mom is on the ceiling—reaching up to me. I reach down to her. She's going away. I want Mom to help save us, but I want her to stay with me, too.

The flight attendant grabs Mom's arm. "For God's sake, hurry! Derrick's blinded! Grey's hurt!"

The pilot. The copilot. Nobody's flying our shuttle.

Mom goes up on tiptoes. She's too short to reach all the way up to hug me. She squeezes the tips of my fingers and says, "I've got a job to do, honey. You be brave, like our hero, okay?"

I nod and try to keep the tears squeezed tight inside. Mom wants me to be brave like Val Thorsten, who laughs in the face of danger.

She turns away. She runs past the hurt people, then runs on the ceiling to the red door into the cockpit.

Smoke comes out when she opens it. She walks right into the smoke and the red door slams shut behind her.

"Go manual!" Val's voice. The volume is so high, the words are like a cuff to the head. They bring me back into the *Squid*. "Go manual!"

"Val! I was with her!"

"Not now, kid. Forty seconds and you'll hit the surface. I've lost the link with your flight transponder. I can't fly it by remote anymore. You've got to take over."

Just like Mom . . . I've got a job to do!

I punch down on the hand controls to snuff the rocket. The astrogator spins and whirls as the *Squid* tumbles right side up, then upside down. I start hitting opposing thrusters, slow the spiral until it damps out like a coin spinning to a stop on a table.

The *Squid* is under control—*my* control.

Val says, "You're dropping too fast."

Only seven hundred feet above the Moon. I kick in the rocket and throttle up to eighty percent to slow my fall, then lay on some thrusters to get my forward speed down.

"Get your forward speed down," Val says, then sees I'm ahead of him. "Nice maneuver. Confirm target."

"Dead ahead, Val." Out the window is a big glittering square—the fence around Tranquility Base.

"Five hundred dropping twenty per second . . . forty forward." Val calls the readings so I can concentrate on managing pitch, roll, and yaw. Was anyone helping Mom? "Slow . . . slower . . ."

I thumb the throttle to ease the descent rate. I don't like what the radar tells me, though. The glitch altered my course enough that I might come down inside the fence. Can't do that! The footsteps. The equipment. The flag. The rocket exhaust will wipe out all that carefully preserved history.

I shove the throttle higher, trying to hover, buy some time. Got to nudge the *Squid* away from here.

"What're you doing?"

The low fuel warning light flashes. Sixty seconds until the descent engine tank is empty.

"Land!" Val yells. "Land!"

I make the *Squid* sweep and bank like a helicopter. It comes broadside to the fence. I ram the throttle to full power.

The *Squid* cartwheels over the fence. A landing strut jolts into the surface. Dust swirls outside the window. The engine coughs. Another jolt. The *Squid* starts to tip over. I fight that with everything the tiny maneuvering thrusters can put out. The engine coughs again. The *Squid* lifts, then comes down hard enough to jam my teeth together.

I kill the power before the rocket sucks up another

drop of fuel. The swirling dust whisks away like a swarm of silvery bees. Without any air to hold it, not a speck lingers to spoil the view.

"Kid, you okay? Respond!" Val doesn't sound calm and professional. "Stewart!"

I'm alive!

I pulled it out!

"Tranquility Base to *Old Glory*." Calm and professional. "The *Squid* has landed."

Val doesn't respond for a second. Then he says, "Smart aleck."

MISSION TIME

T plus 41:11:20

THE view through the tiny window is beautiful and very still. The gently rounded plain of the Sea of Tranquility stretches to the sharply curved horizon. Beyond the crisp white edge of the Moon, space is a jet-black wall—close and huge.

The stillness outside seeps inside me, replacing the adrenaline rush from the wild landing. Tears come, pool, then spill out and run down my cheeks. In the low gravity, they flow thick and slow like the syrup I poured over my birthday waffles yesterday. But oh, these tears are not sweet as, alone on this dead sea, I remember the images from FSF Flight 78 that came to me in the crash-diving squid.

They play before my eyes as if projected on the black lunar sky. And what I did not understand—could not even try to understand in the middle of that crisis—now comes clear to me: *The NewsVid the Counselor kept forcing me to watch is a complete fake.* That's why I never felt the horror of it. I wasn't on the ground with Mark and Dad. I was on the shuttle with Mom.

A sob heaves itself out from deep within my chest.

"What's the matter, Stewart?" Val's voice breaks in like a crack of thunder. "Are you hurt?"

I fight down another sob. "Things keep coming in bits."

A long pause, then Val says harshly: "This is no time for a stroll down memory lane, kid. You've gotta move out."

"All you care about is your stupid mission!"

"Not true, but LunaCom must've seen you scrawling that ship over half the sky. A hopper's bound to be on the way."

A hopper is a fast, spidery runabout used by park rangers. Alldrives has the contract for maintaining the Humanity Parks. The rangers work for them. I've got to get refocused on the mission. Get the VT's NavComp out of here. I'm sure that's what Mom would want me to do.

I swing my feet out the opening, bounce down on my rump, then scoot onto the small step made by the descent stage. It's three feet to the surface from there.

I jump and immediately sense the weird, slow tug of the Moon's gravity compared to Earth's. When I land, my boots sink into the thick layer of dust that covers the surface like frosting. Thousands of tiny grains fly up and make perfect, lazy parabolas before coming down again.

I straighten up and . . . there's the Earth! A crescent-shaped slice of stained glass against the nothingness. It seems just a step beyond the horizon.

I've seen this before! With Mom, at the science museum. There's an entire wall filled with the famous picture, "Earthrise," that Bill Anders took from *Apollo 8*, the first manned ship to orbit the Moon. I remember Mom telling me, "When you stand on the Moon, Stewart, you feel like you can jump from the horizon right into an ocean on Earth."

The view swims in a kind of liquid ripple. I think it's more tears, but then my space suit disappears!

I'm at the space museum, standing with Mom in front of the giant mural of "Earthrise."

My hand reaches toward the beautiful Earth. Fingers touch glass, cool and smooth. My other hand rests in Mom's, warm and comfortable. She finally found the mural she wanted to show me.

"Someday I'll take you there, Stewart."

"Promise?"

"Promise. When you're six. No kids on rockets until they're six. That's my rule."

Silver, like liquid mercury, seems to flow over my bare fingers and I'm back in my suit, back on the Moon, full of new comprehension: The trip was my birthday present! We were coming back from the Moon!

Mark knew! While we looked at this place in the HOOPscope. When I said, "Someday, I'm going there," he knew I already had!

Why would they take all of that away from me?

My heart, so full of the remembered excitement of standing with Mom in the science museum, fills with hurt now. All those years, I could've been remembering . . .

Did we stand right here, together?

I look down. The surface outside the fence is packed down with the footsteps of a million tourists.

"Move it, will ya?" Val snaps. There's a camera on the *Squid.* I must look like a piece of a moon rock, frozen on the spot like a zombie. "Radar confirms there's a hopper on the way. ETA twenty-one minutes."

I've got to get this job done. Get home. Get answers.

That risky cartwheel maneuver dropped me about

a hundred yards outside the fence. The descent stage of the LEM dominates the area inside. Sunlight glitters off the gold foil skirting. The flag with the fake ripple stands next to it, slightly tilted from straight up. Every fold and crinkle, each color, is incredibly clear. Sharper than things look on a perfect summer day.

I almost expect it to flutter.

Calling to mind Val's treasure map instructions, I take a step toward the southwest corner post. The surface seems to flex, like walking on a trampoline, and I feel as if I might spring into the sky at any moment. It's hard to balance, too. Then I remember . . . *hop*. That's the best way to get around on the Moon.

A few bouncy, nearly out-of-control rocking horse hops bring me to the southwest corner post. Stop. Stumble. A little tricky, this Moon walking!

From there, I head out on a 45-degree diagonal for about thirty feet. By the time I plant my feet to stop, I've found my center of balance, made friends with the Moon's weak grip. Activating the locator strapped to my wrist, I pass it over the surface to home in on the bore shell. Little lights tell me hotter or colder, then flash a bull's-eye. A wobbly drop to my knees. I scoop away a few inches of dust. It clings to my gloves like soot.

At the bottom of the hole, a neon bright orange

ribbon lies curled on the hard rock. Leaning far to the side like Val warned me to, I tug it. Dust and shredded packing erupts. The ribbon rips from between my fingers as the end cap rockets out of sight, trailing it.

In its wake, a different, neon bright blue ribbon floats slowly to the surface as if it is sinking through water. Attached to the other end is the NavComp core . . . the brains of one of the most amazing spaceships ever built. A criminal brain. Carefully, I draw it out of the bore tube.

Oh wow!

It slides into the sunlight, three feet of laser-etched microcircuit perfection. The polished surface glitters with color as if inlaid with a million jewels. I have to hate it for what it did to Val, but that was the corrupted programming, not this beautiful machine.

I'm reluctant to touch it with my grimy gloves. Gripping it by the ends, I hop back to the *Squid*. I twist off the big cap from one of the storage tubes and slip the core in. Seal it up. The elapsed timer on the glove says that only took eight minutes. I don't know why he had to hustle me. Lots of time to spare.

Unless he's worried about the oxygen supply. We gained a few more hours than he predicted at midcourse, but there's not enough to get home—not enough, really, to go anywhere.

What's his plan? He has one, I'm sure. Kept secret, as usual. Only way to find out is to finish this.

"NavComp secure, Val. How's that for speedy?"

"One more task, kid."

Uh-oh. A surprise.

"What is it?"

"The moneyman behind this mission wants a souvenir."

Of course! Two tubes. Can't be a spare. Nothing on this mission has a spare. "You want me to grab a rock?"

"No, kid. He's already got rocks. He wants the flag."

"The flag!" I nearly fall down, spinning around to look at it. *That* flag? It's the only real one from the Apollo missions to survive all these years. Taking it would be like stealing Plymouth Rock. I can't believe he just asked me to do that.

"I won't do it, Val. It's stealing."

"How many times have *I* been stolen from, huh, kid? I sacrificed all my life. Made billions for others. And what have I got? The VT sabotaged. Dead crewmembers no one mourns. A lifetime smeared into a few glitzy 3-Vids. Don't talk to *me* about stealing."

Revenge. Justice. It was such a great mission . . .

I'm not mad at him. I hate them—Alldrives, the 3-Vid producers, everyone who left Val grabbing at this rotten lifeline from some sleazy rich collector.

"Move out. You've got ten minutes. And don't think you can come back without that flag. The remote's working good enough for me to keep you grounded."

I stroke a landing strut of my ship. He's taken it back. I look up, searching the blackness for *Old Glory.* Nothing in sight. "You wouldn't strand me here, would you?"

"Try me."

An all-or-nothing mission, isn't that what he said?

I look at the flag. Just a bit of cloth to restore all his old glory . . .

Three short bounces bring me to the fence. When my boot touches the lowest rail, a sign flashes:

PLEASE DO NOT STAND ON THE FENCE.

Alarms must be going off somewhere.

Up another rung. Beyond the fence, the surface is almost pristine, tracked with only a few paths of footprints. No one has ever set foot inside except those two first men on the Moon. Even worse than taking the flag would be to mingle my footsteps with theirs. They risked everything to give us the stars. Their glove-prints are on the flag. Not even Val Thorsten is important enough to ruin that.

I step away from the fence, shuffle back toward the *Squid.*

Val can see that on the camera. He shouts, "No! Go back!"

I don't trust my voice. Just keep marching.

"Kid, please—"

The radio channel shifts. Static, then: "—calling *Old Glory.* At rendezvous, where are you?"

I freeze with one foot on the *Squid*'s ladder. Not Val. Not LunaCom. And not a squiggle. "Who's that, Val?"

"That's our ride out of here, kid. And that flag is our ticket."

The getaway car. Somewhere near, there's a ship, with air. The rich guy's, maybe even a Comet Catcher. Another part of Val's plan finally becomes clear: We were never going back to Earth. So what was going to happen to me?

"Don't just stand there, kid. Time's running out!"

"Time's up," I tell him when, like the cavalry, a hopper appears from behind a huge boulder. "The hopper's here."

"Hustle, you can get it!" He's still trying to save this mission, just like the first time when I messed up in the *Squid*. But I swing up onto the shelf. Disappear from his camera. "Kid, don't do this to me! He won't help us escape if we don't bring him that flag."

"Us? I can go with the rangers."

Silence. I've finally surprised him.

A geyser of dust shoots up as the beetlelike hopper leaps closer. Once, there was nothing I wanted more than to be rescued . . .

Why doesn't he say something? Will he really let it end this way?

I shift on the shelf in front of the hatch to get a better view of the hopper. My elbow bumps the storage tube and it hits me like lightning—I *can't* carry out my threat. Can't let them rescue me. The rangers in that hopper work for Alldrives. They'll get the core!

Twisting, I stick my hands through the hatch and grip the control boxes to haul myself into the *Squid.* My boots are slippery with dust. I'm working up a sweat. When I'm finally in position, the first thing I see is the bright red message—ASCENT ENGINE LOCK OUT.

"Val." My mouth is dry. I swallow hard. "Val, release the engine lock. Or don't. I don't care."

The hopper skips to a stop a dozen yards away. He'd better make his choice fast.

The red light flickers to green. The pins holding the two stages together blast out with an explosive bump. I'm free to fly!

"Okay, kid, we'll do it your way. Can't trust the remote anymore. Bring her up."

The thrill goes straight to my fingertips. I punch

the ignition switch. My head almost pops down through the neck ring as the acceleration jumps massively. I tighten my leg muscles so I'm standing tall. The radar picks up *Old Glory*. Keying in the thrusters, I tweak the *Squid* onto the correct flight path. Adjust ascent rate. Counteract a little excess roll.

Val says, "You've got a little drift there."

I key in a thruster to compensate. When I squeeze the firing button on the joystick, nothing happens. I recycle the thruster twice. No luck.

"Rotate one eighty. Try a different nozzle."

"Right." I key in a 180-degree rotation. It comes off fine. Now I can use a different thruster to correct my course. I activate the new thruster. It fires. Alarm codes start flashing like crazy.

"You're vectoring out!"

I try to shut it off. "The thruster jammed!"

It's fighting against the boost from the ascent engine. If I can't counteract the drag, I won't make it into a stable orbit before the fuel runs out.

"Compensate!"

"I'm trying! Half the thrusters aren't responding. The hard landing damaged something."

The *Squid* fishtails across the sky like a crude bottle rocket. My fingers ache from chasing thruster codes all over the keypad. The scar throbs, threatening to cramp. Somehow, I stay close to on course—

close enough, I hope. The main engine flares out. The tank beneath my feet is empty. The altimeter peaks at fifty miles—way too low to maintain orbit!

The Moon's gravity recaptures the *Squid*. It starts to drop toward the unforgiving surface.

21

MISSION TIME

T plus 41:40:21

VAL! Help!"

But he can't help me because I'm back on the crashing shuttle with Mom . . .

"Lord God hear our prayer . . ." The minister kneels in the aisle with several other passengers. They can do that because Mom got us right side up.

"You must stabilize," Tower Control says. The words coming over the speaker drown out the prayers.

A flight attendant kneels next to my seat. He helps me get an oxygen mask on. A lot of smoke came in when Commander Derrick crawled out of flight deck. A cloth is wrapped around his head and over his eyes. It's stained with blood. He had to feel his way to a seat. That's when the minister started praying.

"Don't they think Mom can save us?"

"Hang in there, kid." The mask makes the flight attendant's voice sound like his nose is pinched. He pats my hand. His fingers are ice cold. "The copilot, Mr. Grey, is in the crawl space trying to get to the broken control cables. He might be right under us."

"Mom's all alone?"

Tower Control says, "We can't give you a dive vector if you don't stabilize."

"I'm flying a stone here . . . wait . . . " Mom says and everyone leans toward the sound of her voice. "Getting some response . . . no, lost it. Copilot's below decks . . . holding things together with his bare hands . . ."

"Ten seconds and you'll be beyond recovery."

Ears covered, an old lady wails, "For God's sake, shut that off!"

She doesn't want to hear Mom's voice. The flight attendant stands up, reaching for the speaker. I grab his hand. "NO!"

The shuttle lurches. The deck pitches upward. The speaker goes sputtery, like a badly tuned radio, then Mom's cry of triumph, "Tower, tower, positive airfoil! I've got control!"

Those remembered words—exactly the same as in the NewsVid—shock me back into my own chaotic world, trapped in a crash-diving squid somewhere above the airless surface of the moon.

They were the last words I ever heard her say.

". . . get control of the ship." Val's voice. Urgent. Commanding. My hero. Mom's hero.

Get control. Mom had to. *I* have to. I look at the instruments. The *Squid*'s in a corkscrew dive forty-five miles above the surface. The fuel ran out before it achieved orbital velocity. It's falling back toward the Moon. Alarm codes flash urgently, calling for the pilot to do something.

Me.

"Stewart! Stabilize your flight path! Respond, damn it!"

"Working on it." I lock in a maneuver . . . fire. The spiral slows. Again. The course I manage to hold is a very steep dive, almost straight down. The surface rushes up at me; details coming clearer and clearer. I ought to be terrified, but I'm not. I've done my job. Only Val can save me now.

I tell him, "Course stable."

"Then here I come," Val calls. The familiar sound of the big main engine roars in my earphones. Val's powering out of orbit. I wish I could see that dive!

Old Glory is a blip on my radar twenty-five miles above and a couple hundred miles ahead of me dropping fast out of its high orbit, but I'm dropping faster every second. Val has to get below the *Squid* and catch it in the cargo canister like an outfielder snagging a high fly. Only thing is, this ball is moving three thousand miles an hour, and is as fragile as an egg.

A sudden lurch sets me struggling to regain control again. When the flurry is over, the faulty thruster has finally run out of propellant.

Val says, "Come about to give visual."

I'll do *anything* so I don't have to keep looking at where I'm going to end up. I backflip the *Squid.* The ashen surface drops from view, replaced with a few glittery stars in a vast blackness—infinite and still. No sense of falling now. *Old Glory* flares across my view, tail first, a blurred whiteness spitting a cone of blue fire. The backward firing rocket slows the shuttle's orbital velocity, causing it to arc steeply toward the surface and—if Val's got the angles right—me.

"I see you!"

"Trajectory match?"

"Not yet."

The capture attempt requires our ships to be on the same path—both crash-diving at a mile a minute!

Like some great spouting whale, gray vapors erupt from the shuttle's thrusters. Val's only using five nozzles out of the dozens dotting the hull. It takes tons of skill to control such a big ship with so few, but without automatic NavComp control, Val would risk getting confused like I did at midcourse.

"All right, Val!"

"Orbital match," he says. "I'm going to pitchover so I can see enough to guide you into the cargo bay."

The blue cone of flame disappears. The shuttle tumbles end over end and gently rolls at the same time. Now the nose is pointing at me. The windows of flight deck flash with reflected sunshine.

Val says, "Final approach. Don't let that thing wobble an inch."

I concentrate on the readouts, punching keys with my knuckles to keep the *Squid* stable. The pain cramping along the scar is so intense I can't uncurl my fingers anymore.

"Steady . . . I'm taking you over the top."

I look out the window into the throat of a forward thruster. The big black nose slips below me. I want Val to hurry, but he's careful, sliding in slow. One bump could knock the *Squid* hopelessly out of reach. The hull near the cockpit fills my window. Every other tile is missing. The shuttle shifts. I can see into flight deck. Val hunches close to the displays. One of us is upside down.

He glances at me. We could shake hands.

Then the cockpit's white roof spreads below me. Only a few feet to go. I strain to see forward. What's that? A blurred darkness looms ahead. Another memory coming? Then I realize I'm seeing the end of the docking ring sticking above the hull. The *Squid*'s going to hit it!

"Val! The dock!"

A garbled curse punches my ears. The shuttle drops away. Too slow. The *Squid*'s nose rams the docking ring hard. Metal collapses, shoving the window at me. The glass shatters into crazed spiderweb patterns. My head bobs, jamming my mouth against the helmet rim. The pain is nothing next to the way my guts knot as the *Squid* begins to somersault like a gymnast soaring over a vaulting horse.

He's going to lose me! "Come up!"

The shuttle surges, scooping the *Squid* into the canister. The *Squid* hits the rear wall. The reaction force causes the crumpled nose to lift. It's the start of a tumble that will toss me out over the tail.

"Nose down!" Val yells. "Nose down!"

I'm already working the forward thrusters, shoving the nose to the floor of the canister. The *Squid* bounces off the rear wall, rakes along the canister, and rams the air lock hatch. Sledgehammers come down on my shoulders. Somehow, I manage to hit the rear thrusters in time to stop another rebound.

"I'm in!"

A strong acceleration surges along my body as the shuttle's main rocket blasts us out of the crash dive. Its power rattles the shuttle, rattles the *Squid,* rattles my head.

The rocket shuts down, leaving a hiss in the sudden quiet.

At first, I think it's just noisy headphones.

Bing bing bing.

The suit alarm. Puncture! That's air! Mine!

"I'm losing air!"

"I read it. Don't panic. It's small. You're just a few feet from the air lock. You'll be fine."

It's amazing how much more powerful his words are than the sound of the escaping air. Too bad he's wrong. "I'm closer than that."

"Say again?"

"The *Squid* hit the hatch." I bite out the words, trying to hold my breath and talk at the same time.

"Hold on." The controls set in the bulkhead start blinking as Val tries to cycle the hatch. The hatch moves a fraction of an inch and . . . stops.

"Val, it's jammed!"

A loud pop. Pressure builds painfully against my eardrums. The emergency air reserve floods the suit in a single rush. Buys me some time. Once only.

"Hang in there, kid!" The channel shifts. "Mayday.

Mayday. Astronaut in trouble. Suit puncture. Trapped on EVA. I'm coming down."

Shifting accelerations tug at me. The *Squid* rocks and slides. "It's moving!"

"Get out. I'll dump her!"

"No. You'll lose the core!"

"Forget it. Just get out!"

I swing my legs through the door. Curling my fingers under the hand control boxes, I pull. Gravel slides beneath my shoulder blade. Hurts so much I scream.

"What's going on?"

"Hurt . . ." I clamp my teeth together. Pull. I pop out, flail to grab hold of the storage tube bracket. Clutch it fiercely.

The *Squid* tilts, rolls me toward the deck. Stops just before it squashes me. Hurry! My glove slips on the cap of the tube holding the VT's NavComp core.

"Are you out?"

"Retrieving . . . core . . ." The cap seemed so easy to turn before. The muscles in my arm burn. Need more air. Breathe deep. The air seems so thick.

The cap drops off. The core slips out. Catch it. Snug it under the suit harness. Kick free to fall onto the anchor boom. Arms and legs wrap around it, a fierce clench.

"Clear!"

Vapor from a thruster washes over me. The *Squid* rolls horribly, like a dead fish in an ocean swell. Another blast sends it spilling out of the canister, tumbling toward the surface and destruction. I feel stricken with loss, but Val had to do it, otherwise it might've crushed me rolling around in here.

Good-bye, *Squid*. A gray fog seems to hide it from view as a musty smell fills my suit, like in a cellar; moist and stale. Some kind of bellows puffs near me. It makes a desperate dragging, sucking sound. Someone should fix it so I can hear Val better. Or is that LunaCom?

"—coming too fast!"

". . . rockets . . ."

"Pull up! Go long!"

"No . . . you won't get the kid in time."

". . . base . . . soft soil . . ."

"Kid?"

That's me. Val's talking to me. Wish he'd speak up.

"Stewart! Breathe slower. Stop gulping."

The noise is me!

"Slow . . . slower . . . In. Now out," Val urges. It's nice to obey him. The grayness clears away. My breathing quiets to soft puffs.

"I . . . feel . . . better . . ."

"Good. You have to work fast. We're going to hit very hard. Get into the shock webbing. Understand?"

The shock webbing hangs at the back of the canister. I focus on it through the pink mist of blood and spittle smearing my visor. I don't want to let go of the boom. "It's . . . so . . . far . . ."

"It's your only chance."

I pull my interlocked fingers apart to let go of the boom. Sharp pain stabs between my shoulder blades.

"Secure?"

"Just . . . started . . ." Grab the first handhold. The next a foot away. Chest heaves. Nothing to breathe. Hurts. Better lie here . . . rest . . .

"Thirty seconds until impact." Val's voice goes flat—calm and professional.

I reach. Another handhold. So many more to go . . . but then even this present peril cannot save me from the pull of the past . . .

"We can't confirm gear down!" Tower Control shouts, losing their cool for the only time in the crisis.

I know what that means—no wheels. Everyone else does, too. People start screaming.

"We've spread foam," Tower Control says. "Good luck."

"Crash procedures!" Commander Derrick bellows over

the noise. Even though he can't see, his voice still snaps
with the power of command.

It scares me. Scares the flight attendants, who hop to
attention, call out, "Everyone—sit! Get pillows! Get
buckled up!"

The attendants don't have to worry about me. I've
been a good boy.

I hear the air rushing outside and the faint rumble of
thrusters. I listen hard for each different pulse, because
Mom is making that happen and the copilot, too, some-
where under the floor.

The seat kicks me. There's a great tear and roar
and . . .

Onelastpullfor Mom.

Impact.

The shuttle compresses, then springs apart. Heat
tiles shoot overhead like missiles. Great geysers flare
up from the thrusters. The force of the crash drives me
toward the deck. The webbing digs and claws
and bites.

Smoke everywhere. People running. I run. Push them.
Shove them. Everyone's trying to escape. Not me.

"Mom!"

I grab the emergency handle on the red cockpit door.

Skin smokes. A smell like barbecue. Strong hands grab me. Pull me away. Fight them!

"Mom! Mom!"

I'm carried away from her, fast, faster . . .

"Mom! Mom!"

I call and call and call until there's no air left in my suit to scream with anymore.

22

MISSION TIME
T plus 51:32:22

MY eyes flutter against a harsh light.

A big room. Bare ceiling miles away. White, clean walls. I'm on my back. There's a small control panel on the wall behind my head. Everything's too neat. Too far away. I remember a smaller place, dim and comfortably crowded with old things. The noises are all wrong here. Sharp pulses and beeps and what's that? A sputtering, crackling sound like static, getting louder: rushing, now roaring—

DECOMPRESSION!

"Val! Val!" My chin rubs against something smooth around my neck. "Val!"

"Shhh. Stewart. Shhh."

Dad's voice. His face appears close above me, interrupting the light.

"Dad, oh Dad, he's dead."

"Calm down, he's okay." Dad sits on the edge of the bed. The room goes all angles as my body tilts toward him. But I can't *feel* the change. He lifts one of my hands into his, but he might as well be picking up a stick.

"I can't feel!"

Dad touches my cheek. "Feel that?"

I nod.

"You're in an Immobilizor. You broke your collarbone." Dad traces a finger across the white yoke below my chin. The complete rig looks like a chest plate from a suit of medieval armor. "You're one big bruise from head to toe."

But I'm alive! I strain to see the Immobilizor better. There's a big lump below my nose. Fat lip. If I'm this beat up . . . "What about Val?"

"Broke his arm falling to the lower deck." The way Dad says it, you can hear the wish that it was worse. "He panicked and jumped straight from the pilot seat to the air lock to escape the decompression. The old fool forgot he was on the Moon."

"Val didn't panic." He rode it out until the last possible moment, then dove through the floor hatch to middeck, just like we'd done a hundred times during the trip. It's the fastest way. Just a little too fast with gravity helping.

Mom rode it out, but she had nowhere to jump.

Something around my heart crumples. "All those years, Dad, I thought Mom had screwed up. But I understand now. She rode it out to save me."

"Ohmygod!" Dad pulls back from me and looks across the room. "He's remembered!"

Someone else is here. I crane my head, catch a glimpse of shimmering light in the corner. Oh no!

"Hello, Stewart." Mrs. Phillips's voice comes out of the shimmer. It approaches the bed.

"Get away! I won't let you make me forget again!"

But how can I stop them? They can do anything to me while I'm like this.

"Be calm, Stewart. I'm really me this time, not the Counselor." The shimmer stops at the foot of the bed. It resolves into a hologram of Mrs. Phillips. On Earth, she's in a holochamber, navigating a virtual reality re-creation of this hospital room. "Please, don't worry. That will never be done to you again."

"Is that true, Dad?" I look at him sitting beside me. He's slumped and far away, paying attention to some private thought. I haven't forgotten anything the Counselor said. Dad's the one who gave permission. "Dad? You're going to undo the mnemonic suppression, aren't you? I'll be able to do AstroNav, won't I?"

"That stupid AstroNav!" Dad jumps up from the bed and keeps going, crashes into the ceiling. The light panel thumps and clatters. For an instant, his feet dangle near my head, then he settles to the floor. Look who forgot about gravity! Moon gravity.

Dad curses, rubbing his head while digging into a pants pocket. He pulls out a piece of paper.

"It's all because of this, isn't it!" Dad waves the application to Space Academy Camp in my face. "Some crazy idea to bring it to me."

"Your note with the 3-Vid, that pilot you met . . . you said I should stick to fantasies. I had to do something!"

"That's no excuse! How could you get into a rocket with that man!" There's venom in the way he says "that man." He really does hate Val.

"I didn't know who he was."

"Even worse! A drunk! A stranger! He almost killed you!"

My brain shrugs even if my shoulders won't. "The booster problem wasn't his fault."

"You're protecting him?"

"He didn't do anything wrong."

Dad stares at me. "He *kidnapped* you!"

"No he didn't."

Mrs. Phillips comes around the bed. Stands between me and Dad, facing him. "Ted, this is not the approach we discussed."

"You stay out of this. He needs to understand how

dangerous that man is." Dad steps right through her. "Why did you come to the Moon, Stewart?"

Dad's so wild. I can't imagine what he wants me to say. Out of all the reasons, I pick the one that drove me hardest. "To escape the Counselor."

"Not this time. The trip with your mother. What were you doing here?"

"I thought it was my birthday trip, because I was six."

"That was an excuse. You came because of that man! To help him hide his stuff from Alldrives. She set up a secret hideout on the dark side for him to use when he finally got back. Don't you understand, Stewart? He was still millions of miles away—months of travel still to go. But she got that secret message and jumped into action. *Anything* for Val Thorsten. If she'd listened to me, waited awhile, you would never have been on that shuttle. She'd be alive!"

Dad's words come like a dam burst and I'm left grasping at facts, trying to make sense of what he's said. I can't. Except one thing: there's a secret hideout somewhere that Val never used. Mom died before she could tell him about it.

"Val didn't make Mom come to the Moon, you just said it yourself. It was her decision. It's crazy to blame him." I look past Dad to Mrs. Phillips for help. "Isn't it?"

She stands frozen, observing Dad. The sight jolts me. Dad's her client, too. She isn't here just for me. She says, "This is completely unconstructive. Forget Val for now, Ted. Talk to Stewart. Tell him."

Her words scare me. I thought I'd remembered the worst already. "Tell me what?"

Dad clams up, turns his back to us.

Mrs. Phillips walks through Dad and comes to stand on the opposite side of my bed.

"I'm sorry I hurt you and then ran away."

"You were understandably distraught." She casts a glance over to Dad, then looks down at me with sad, tired eyes. "Many mistakes have been made recently. Ted, please, speak of Margaret. It's time."

Dad turns. His cheeks are moist with tears. "All these years, I've wanted to tell you so many things, Stewart, but I—"

"Wait. You *wanted* to tell me things? I thought you wanted me to forget!"

Dad sniffs and wipes his tears away with the back of his hand. He bows his head. "You wouldn't heal. You were . . . stuck . . . in the accident. Mark and I, we couldn't put your mother to rest."

"I don't remember any of that. I remember someone pulling me away from the cockpit. I remember screaming for Mom. When I try to look forward from that moment, nothing comes."

Mrs. Phillips says, "We will . . . fix that. Recovery of all your memories will not be entirely pleasant. But the good will return with the bad."

"I'm not afraid. You've got to hang on to memories even if they hurt."

"But that's how we lost you, Stewart!" Dad says. "You kept reliving the accident. Over and over again. It was horrible."

"Out there with Val . . . when he drank, he remembered all the bad stuff. He went on and on. I just wanted him to shut up. Was it like that for you and Mark?"

Dad bites his lower lip. Nods, then looks away. "We wanted to be able to live a normal life. The price to help you this way was high. We had to move. We stuck to the false stories so we wouldn't trigger your memories. Some of the real Margaret . . . faded with the pretending. But you lost the most."

"So it's true. The Counselor took away my memory."

"Something like that," Mrs. Phillips says. "Using mnemonic suppression was a desperate and, perhaps, not so wise choice. I blame myself for what happened with the Counselor. Your recent dreams revealed that the suppression was failing. That horrible NewsVid is a reinforcer. We had to make you watch it, but I couldn't administer the treatment myself. I left the dirty work to the Counselor. The task challenged its programming because in the past few weeks, we'd been preparing you to *reclaim* the memories. But your father . . . he needed more time."

"So that's what you postponed and why Mark was so upset."

"Yes," Dad says. "Mark's been desperate to end this whole thing."

"Is Mark okay? Can we call him?"

"Sure." Dad swings the wall-mounted comm-unit over the bed. "Keep it light for now. I don't think he's slept since you died . . . I mean, disappeared."

As he dials, he leans heavily on the unit. Dark circles surround his eyes. He hasn't slept, either. Mrs. Phillips's eyes are staring and blank. Neither has she.

I thought I'd hate them. I thought I'd never forgive them for taking Mom away, for all those hopeless hours trying to do AstroNav. But they were trying to protect me. Val was, too. He knew, at the end of the memories, Mom was dead.

Mark stares out of the screen at me with a huge, goofy grin spread across his ashen face. He looks even worse than Dad. Behind him, Andrea is sprawled on the workroom sofa, asleep. Her hair hangs to the floor.

"Hey, Stub," Mark says.

"Hey yourself." My eyes focus back on the foreground of the picture. Next to his computer terminal is a plate with dark crumbs on it. "Is that my birthday cake?"

"Oh, yeah, was anyway. It was already in the oven when the police showed up. The second I saw the picture of Val, I knew you weren't dead. Not with Val Thorsten flying that thing."

Mark believes in Val, too!

"I got right to work looking for you. Someone real good was helping Val hide. I didn't sort through all the red herrings covering the shuttle's trail until you were headed down in that fish—"

"Squid."

"Whatever."

"What did you think of my landing?"

Mark shakes his head. "I thought of your stupid simulations and the sound of crashing."

"Oh. I'm better than that now. I learned a lot from Val."

"Figures. Mom always said—" Mark hesitates over the forbidden words.

"It's okay," I say quickly. "I'm remembering. I know he was her teacher at Space Academy. I know she worked for Thorsten Engineering."

"Really?" Mark glances left and right at the adults crowded near the headboard. "Is it really okay?"

"Emotions are a bit raw," Mrs. Phillips says, "but we're stumbling along fairly well."

"Then it's over." Mark's voice thickens with emotion. "It's been . . . I've . . . It's like we've been in a witness protection program all these years."

Then he laughs. "All those years sheltering you from associative triggers and who do you ship out with? The real Val Thorsten. The perfect trigger."

"I thought he was lying to me. He's nothing like the guy in the 3-Vids."

"You can say that again," Mark says. "He's one scary man! Always playing some angle to get money for that stupid ship of his. Always trying to strap me into *something*!"

It finally sinks in. Mark *knows* Val personally. He must have gone to work with Mom sometimes and . . . oh, wow! They were building the Valadium Thruster. "Did you ever see the VT? Were you ever *inside* it?"

Mark laughs. "Sure."

"You lucky stiff!"

"I'll tell you all about it when you get home. I can't wait to tell you everything!" Mark smiles and shakes his head slowly. "By the way, what *was* Val up to this time?"

The core! What happened to it? I don't dare ask. I'm not sure if TIA is on the Moon, but certainly it's

there with Mark, so I only say, "Can't seem to remember right now."

But my mind is racing. I strapped the core tight
against my suit, then . . . I don't remember anything
after the shuttle hit. Did the rangers rescue us or people from LunaCom? Could Alldrives have it? The mission would be a complete failure if that happened!
I've got to talk to Val. But I disobeyed him, left the
flag behind. Will he talk to me?

"Later, then," Mark says, so chill. He loves intrigue.
"Guess I'll sign off. You take it easy, Stub."

"No other choice with this thing around my neck!"

"Hey, Dad. I hate to say it, but I told you so. I think
he deserves an apology. Bye."

The screen goes dark. Dad swings the unit back to
the wall.

"What did Mark mean about an apology?"

Dad slouches against the wall, far away from me.
Mrs. Phillips stays out of sight, but I can almost feel
her intensity, expecting something to happen.

Dad sighs. "You were never going to need camp,
Stewart. You could do AstroNav in your crib. The skill
would've come back with your memories."

"I wondered. Mom mentioned that in her journal."

"Her journal?" Dad lurches away from the wall.

"He carries that around with him? He showed it to you?"

"No. I read it without his permission. Did Mom keep a copy? Do you have one?"

"Yes. Saved with some other things for you. Maybe it's good that you've seen it. Maybe it'll help you understand what I've been struggling with."

"It had a lot in it."

That doesn't please him, not one bit. "I'll tell you why I had to come to the Moon, Stewart. I came to find my nerve. The nerve to let you go like I used to let Margaret go. You can't know how hard that is to do, when you love someone so much . . . when you . . . need them, and they might never come back."

I *do* understand. Sort of. I felt—abandoned—while reading the journal, when she didn't even mention me for a whole year. But Dad doesn't need me the way he needed Mom, and he did let her go, many times.

I don't want to hurt him, but I have to know if he'll let me go now, too. "Did you find your nerve?"

"You're a piece of work." Dad laughs, but not a real happy laugh. "When I saw the NewsVid of that capsule burning up . . . I couldn't go back and face reentry . . . not right away . . . that's why I'm still here on the Moon."

He's afraid of this life I want. I feel bad, because there's something solid as a stone in me. Whether he finds his nerve or not, it won't matter. "I'm sorry, Dad. I'm going to be a pilot. I *am* a pilot."

"I know, Stewart. I saw you out there." Dad sounds sad, but after a moment, a small smile comes. "You should have seen their faces in the control room when you flipped that thing over the fence. They couldn't believe their eyes! Of course, they'd never seen Margaret fly. She had a special skill—grace, really. Terrified as I was, I recognized that same quality in you."

He really *is* proud of me. And Mom, too!

Dad seems hurt and vulnerable, standing there staring into his clasped hands. I want to hug him. But I can't. I have only words.

"Dad. Thanks for telling me. It's the best birthday present ever."

The Immobilizor chirps and hums, a friendly sound in the comfortable silence. The machine is busy knitting bones, soothing bruises. Dad doesn't seem all pinched up anymore, just exhausted. He sways slightly on his feet. Mrs. Phillips leans against the wall, her arm disappearing into it—a misalignment in the holoprojector. They're falling asleep. I'm wide awake.

I clear my throat, sure I'm about to throw a spark in a fuel tank. "I'd like to see Val."

Dad goes rigid. He glares at me. He's about to say

"no," then stops himself. "A mission isn't complete without a debriefing, huh? Just promise you won't fly away with him. I'd like to get reacquainted with the boy who remembers my wife."

"Sure, Dad. I want that, too."

"I'm glad to hear it." Dad ruffles my hair, then smooths it down, neat. "I'll tell the nurse you want to see him."

When Dad leaves, Mrs. Phillips peels herself out of the wall. "You're father just made a big step toward healing. And you, you seem remarkably accepting of all this."

"I'm not freaking out, am I?" I can call to mind the bits and pieces of my life with Mom that I remembered during the trip in *Old Glory*; all of the details about FSF Flight 78, but none of it comes blasting in on me. No more squiggles.

"I think I'm okay *because* I remembered. Without Mom's example, I might not have survived out there."

I know something else, maybe closer to the real reason, but I'm not going to tell Mrs. Phillips. Mom wasn't a failure. Val taught me that: The best don't always make it home.

"Her final gift," Mrs. Phillips says, losing her calm and professional tone. The hologram flickers, then disappears.

23

DEBRIEFING

WILL Val come? The worry grabs me, but my body can't tense up. Weird. What if he won't come? He doesn't have to see me ever again. Time really drags when all you can do is stare at the ceiling and listen to medical monitors.

The door slides open. Because of the Immobilizor, I can only see the top half of the door frame. No one is there. "Val?"

"Yeah, it's me, kid."

I strain my neck to see. He's in an airchair. A small Immobilizor covers his left forearm. An ugly smear of plastiskin goes from his forehead, over his nose, across his right cheek, and down the side of his neck. The jacket lays across his lap. The duffel hangs from the back. Everything Val owns is on that chair. Including the core?

I know better than to ask. TIA may be watching us.

Val works the joystick on the armrest. The chair glides up to the side of the bed on a cushion of air.

"That looks like fun. Wonder if I'll get one?"

Val grunts. "This is quite a comedown for a guy who nearly hit the speed of light."

"What happened to your face?"

"Bit of window." Val shrugs. "And you?"

"Broken collarbone."

"When you hit the dock." Val looks dissatisfied. Maybe he blames himself for forgetting the docking ring was sticking out. "You've got guts, kid. I thought the core was a goner, but you stuck with the mission."

"Val! What about . . . you know." I roll my eyes, aiming them into corners to remind him about cameras and mikes.

"It's okay, kid. We can talk about that part of the mission."

Not the flag. Not Mom's secret hideout. I wonder if I'll know where it is when I get all my memories back? A sudden sense of excitement grips me. What else will I discover about my life that I don't know I know?

"Soon as I was sure you were okay, I took the core to a judge. My arm broke, my face streaming blood, I got it into court custody. It's been copied and certified and locked up for evidence. Gonna be like a supernova in the aerospace universe, kid. Everyone will know the Valadium Thruster wasn't a failure. Restore my reputation. Good times will come again."

"I want to be part of them, Val."

His expression sours and, turning his face away, he says, "I don't know, kid."

The words come soft, wistful even, but they hit me like the end of the world. He doesn't want me! I wrecked his mission and now I'm off the team. Val Thorsten never did tolerate screwups.

"Have you seen *Old Glory*?" A tight, stricken voice, coming at me with no connection I can figure, as usual.

"No."

The airchair whooshes. Val maneuvers around to the other side of the bed. He backs into the space between the bed and the wall, pulling up next to my pillow. We're close together again, just like aboard the shuttle. I expect him to show me a picture, but instead he presses a button on the wall. A shutter slides away from a big window. Across a flat plain, harshly lit by slanting sunshine, lies the shuttle. It looks huge, even half buried in moon dust. Debris litters a wide area around it. The hull is cracked in a dozen places.

"It really is space junk now," Val says. His mouth draws into a thin line. I don't share his sadness. It was *always* space junk to me.

With his good hand, he roots into a jacket pocket. Is he reaching for some booze?

He lays a fragment of heat shield tile from the shuttle and a shiny, crinkled bit of metal on my pillow. A squiggly line made by a marking pen is on the metal. It's from the *Squid.*

"They found the *Squid* in a crater. I had a friend salvage that bit for you. The old-timers who flew the first airplanes, the barnstormers, they had a tradition. When a pilot went in, and lived, they always saved a bit of the canvas for a souvenir."

An image comes: The *Squid,* her nose smashed, hull dented, rolling like a beached fish. My first ship. I lost her. A sniffle catches at the back of my throat. I start coughing. Val grabs the water bottle. He sticks the water tube between my lips . . . squeezes hard. I pull my mouth away, spluttering.

"You'll drown me!"

Val mops up the spill. "What's the matter?"

"I'm just remembering . . ." The whole mission cascades through my mind like a private 3-Vid. An avalanche of memories hits; the fear, the anger, the fights, midcourse, Val powering out of orbit, the crash . . . Mom . . .

Val's eyes narrow. "Should I call the Counselor?"

"No! They're my memories. I'm keeping them."

"What makes you so sure you can handle them?"

There's challenge, and maybe bitterness, in Val's voice.

"I'm not sure, exactly. I guess I saw her before, I mean in the Counselor's version, making a mistake . . . a failure. But now I know the truth." I feel the tears coming as I organize in my mind and heart the last thing Mom would have thought of. "She was worried the automatic grounding thrusters would fail. So she stayed at the controls to make sure they worked. A choice, not a mistake. She rode it out for me, for everyone."

"Like Tony. Like Bob," Val says, sad.

Things are so different now. I know what he means, what he sees and feels, when he turns inward to that memory. Val and I aren't separated by this mist of make-believe anymore. And even though I wouldn't get that flag for him, he rode it out for me.

"Like you, Val."

Val reaches out and strokes my head, once, rough and awkward. "I tell ya, kid. The best of us don't always make it."

"Yeah." I sniff and he sniffs and we both look away from each other toward the wreck of *Old Glory.*

Eventually, he says, "There'll be an inquiry. Good thing we didn't complete the whole mission, the way it turned out."

"Sure is!" Imagine getting caught with that flag.

But now the rich collector who financed the trip won't get any return on his investment. "What about the expenses?"

"I'll have more than enough to repay expenses once Alldrives settles up. I'm more worried about the kidnapping charge."

"I told Dad you didn't kidnap me. I'll tell the court that, too, if I have to."

Val considers this. "In that case, I should get off with only a few months in jail."

"Jail!"

"I've done worse time, you know that." He looks out at the stars. There's Cassiopeia, the constellation Mom saw from the beach the day they canceled the official search for Val. How many times did she look at the stars, wondering, hoping?

"No booze in jail. Maybe I'll write my memoirs. Set the record straight."

He's sitting here full of his own new hopes because of Mom. "Dad blames you for Mom's death."

"Sometimes I blame myself, kid, crazy as that is. So don't be too hard on your dad, okay?"

I nod even though I don't really understand what would make either of them feel that way.

Val sighs, then gets a look of deep remembering. "I'll never forget how she came strutting into my AstroNav tutorial, confident as you please. She was shorter even than you. Had that coiled copper hair. All attitude, your mom, even as a freshman. Set my back up, until I saw what she could do . . ."

First year at Space Academy. Mom would've been fourteen, a year older than me. He knew her longer than any of us!

Val looks at me, blinks. "And now here you are."

"Dad wants me to stay away from you. He says you're dangerous."

"What do you think?"

"I'm with you!"

He frowns. "We screwed up out there. It's not supposed to be that exciting. You train and prepare so things go along smooth and dull. Most pilots run a tourist liner to Mars. Or haul ore."

"Now you sound like Dad. No way I'm going to haul ore!"

"I figured," Val says, nodding. "We need a star drive, kid. That's the next step for our kind."

"Do you think it'll happen?"

"There are a few possibilities. One thing's certain. If you aren't a rocket pilot, and one of the best at that, you won't ever get the chance."

Val's already given me a better chance than I ever had before. "If you coach me, I could be the best. Will you?"

"I'd like that, kid." There's a yearning in his voice.

Mark sounds that way when he discovers a really neat new code, or Dad when he finds an amazing new electronics circuit. It's an eagerness to get down to work with something new and wonderful. "But you shouldn't be associated with me if you want to get into Space Academy."

"Why?"

He looks into his lap. The eagerness slips behind a mask as slick as the plastiskin. "Alldrives owns the place. It'll blow your whole career if they know we're a team."

"Then I won't go! You can teach me everything."

Val considers, then shakes his head. "No. You have to go to Space Academy. You'd never get a decent job."

"I don't want a decent job. I want to *do* something!"

"Like go to Pluto?"

"Yeah. But how? There's no ship."

He looks straight at me. The harsh light bleaches his eyes to the palest blue, like the Moon in a daytime sky. "Oh, that's right. Lost in the sun. I never could keep those 3-Vids straight."

His words are like our own secret code. Of course Val Thorsten would never let the Valadium Thruster fall into the sun! Not *that* ship!

Hide everything! That was the plan he and Mom

made. I didn't understand before. He meant the Valadium Thruster, too! He used the lifeboat as a decoy. He made the last bit of his trip back to Earth in it and left the VT out there somewhere, parked, just like in my wildest dreams.

"You mean—"

"One step at a time, kid." He silences me. "Let's get you through Space Academy first."

I can only nod. Always a surprise. Like when I first met him. I'm back on Pad 12 and he's thrown open that tiny hatch to unknown adventure again . . .